WAR OF THE

SHADOWS

BOOK ONE OF THE
MISAKIN CHRONICLES

AMBER P. DAVIDSON

SILENT E PUBLISHING

Silent E Publishing Company
4446 Hendricks Ave, #141
Jacksonville, Florida, USA
All Rights Reserved.

ISBN-10 1-941091-06-7
ISBN-13 978-1-941091-06-7

First Edition
10 9 8 7 6 5 4 3 2 1

Acknowledgements

There are so many people that I would like to thank. Thank you to my family. April, you are my best friend, and I'm so lucky to have you as my sister. Mike and Shane, you are the best "brothers" a girl could have. Mom and Dad, thank you for all of your support for my crazy quirks and ideas throughout the years. Thank you for loving me because of my weirdness, not just in spite of it. Thank you to my work families for putting up with me while I worked on this. Thank you, George, for working with me through this process and helping me get here now; my apologies for the procrastination. Finally, to the countless others that I owe thanks to, you're all amazing and I love you.

World War III is happening, but the factions in this war are the creatures of our nightmares. Innocent people are getting caught in the crossfire while the battle of good versus evil truly begins. One woman begins a journey through her own dark past, the present, and the future. Through strange fate she becomes civilization's only hope for survival, or the instrument of its destruction. Let the battle begin. Alexandria Bennett, Alex as she prefers to be called, is a practical woman. When she starts to see unbelievable things happening in her world, she seeks out the one person who seems to have all the answers to learn the truth. But the truth is that Alex knows far more than she believes. She must face the darkness in her own past to learn the truth about who, and what, she is. When her heart is tested by a dangerous enemy, she must make a choice. Will she be tempted by the lure of the darkness, or will her humanity prevail?

Table of Contents

Chapter One: The Reshaping Begins

It started off small, every single abandoned building burned to the ground with nothing but the smell of burning wood and debris. The haze of ash lingered in the air as far as the eye could see. The suspicious thing about it was they all burned down on the same day and there was nothing left once the fires were out. Firefighters could do nothing to control the flames; water, fire extinguishers, even flour, when they got desperate, did nothing to contain them. The news reported nothing but rumors and theories with a lot of emphasis on insurance fraud, but there was no evidence to scavenge through.

Then a battle was caught on an iPhone and no one believed it was insurance fraud anymore. The sky was hazy, with ash still alive in the air, distorting the images late at night, but the battle appeared to be dragons fighting men high in the night sky. Some had wings and some were lifted up on glowing discs of light. There were hundreds on either side battling with swords, talons, teeth, and there was no other word for it... it was magic. Strange lights flew back and forth sending bodies on either side plummeting to the earth. The video lasted all of two minutes before the camera wielder and the spectators around him were blasted by a misfired stream of magic.

Alex was sitting on the couch at her best friend Sierra's home that morning when the video was shown. Once the light came toward the camera in the video, the screen went black. The power shut down in the house, all except for the television. Alex heard neighbors cry out in fear. The screen in front of her turned blue, and the President appeared on the screen.

"Change. What I ran my campaign on. What I ran my Presidency on, has finally begun. Citizens of the United States of America, I know you are frightened by what you have seen recently. There are still more changes to come. Our future will be brighter and safer once this Reshaping is complete. There are enemies coming for us, not just America and her citizens, but our entire civilization. Enemies that we have heard whispers of in the dark but have never known. Enemies that are beyond our ability to fight or defeat. They are coming and will be here soon. This is why changes are necessary as it determines our survival as a species.

"It has been my honor and privilege to serve this great country, but my time as its Commander in Chief is over. The time has come for stronger leadership. For this reason, I and my successors have stepped down from our posts. Thank you for allowing us to serve you, America. We wish for your health, happiness, and safety as we face our new future." He stepped away from the microphone and gestured someone off camera forward.

He had slightly shaggy, ebony-colored hair. His eyes were an icy, bright blue hue, clear and honest. He appeared to be around 30 years old. His nose was slightly crooked on the bridge, as though it had been broken before, but it still seemed perfectly proportioned to his high cheekbones and strong jaw. Alex was shocked because she recognized him. He used to come into the bar where she worked. He always sat well away from everyone and didn't talk or drink very much. She focused as he stepped up to the podium.

He placed his hands on both sides of the podium with his fingers curled at the edges. He looked tall and imposing, but his eyes remained gentle as he began to speak. "Friends and citizens, I know that you are frightened and very confused about what is happening. You must have many questions. One question that you may have is probably the most troubling one: Is this the end of the world? I can tell you that this is exactly what we are trying to prevent. The world is currently undergoing a Reshaping.

"For so long we have been disconnected from each other, but in order to protect innocent lives this has to change now. Transports will be available shortly to take you to protected cities that will have the proper defenses to keep you safe. These cities will not only provide the space you need but also the united front that we need for our survival. We are stronger united than apart and alone. Initially your basic needs will be provided for, and once the first wave of attack has passed, we will all work together within these communities to establish jobs for every able-bodied person. Jobs will be based on our strengths and weaknesses in order to ensure our safety. These cities will be strongly guarded from attack, but the areas outside of these protections will be extremely vulnerable.

"These next few days will bring the final, drastic changes to the Reshaping. This change in leadership scares you, I know, but let me try to ease your fears. All people around the globe, every country and territory, every individual, is receiving a similar message at this time." Sierra grabbed onto Alex's hand as though it were a life raft, and Alex saw that her friend was barely holding it together. She squeezed her hand in reassurance and tuned back to the speech. "... have been protecting you since long before this generation. Now is the time to act. We have a very small window before our enemies attack again, in ever increasing numbers.

"United we will stand and prevail. Our future will be bright, but first we must stand together. Go to the protected cities. If you choose to join in the fight, then we will teach you how to fight these enemies. If you do not wish to fight, then we will provide a safe environment. Go now to the transports. I will reach out to you again soon."

The television died at the end of the transmission and the quiet was overwhelmingly eerie. There was no hum of electricity sparking through the air. She turned to Sierra and saw that her friend was absolutely terrified and heading into shock. Alex grasped her shoulders to get her to focus. Sierra met her eyes, and her tears quietly streamed down her cheeks.

"Sierra, you have to go to the transport. Don't be afraid. I'll figure out what is going on and I will find you." Alex said.

"No! Please don't leave me, I won't know what to do. You're the strong one. I need help, I don't understand what's happening!" Sierra was getting worked up.

"I don't know either, Sierra, but I know someone who does. I will find him and get our answers and then I will come back to you. I promise, but I need to know that you're safe. You're my best friend," she hugged her tight "I **have** to know that you're safe." She suddenly heard what sounded like a helicopter landing. She pulled Sierra with her to the window.

What had landed in the middle of the street was like no helicopter that she had ever seen. There were eight rotor blades at the top of the transport, and it appeared to be in the same sleek silver design as a bullet. As she watched, the entire side of the airborne vehicle was lowered to the ground like a ramp. There was seating for at least a thousand people. People started to leave the homes around them carrying bags and pets, heading toward the transport. Two people stopped near the ramp and waited.

"Time to go," Alex said, and Sierra nodded as she wiped the tears from her cheeks.

"Please be safe, Alex, and don't put yourself in danger," Sierra said.

As Alex opened her mouth to protest, Sierra said, "Don't you look at me like that, Alexandria Renee Bennett! Keep yourself alive and come back to me. I'll stick with my neighbors until we see each other. You know, the newlyweds," They rolled their eyes at each other, and Alex was glad for the lightening of the mood. The neighbors had gotten back from their honeymoon three weeks before. They seemed to think they were still honeymooning, and Sierra had very thin walls. It had made for awkward movie nights lately.

Sierra hugged her tight one more time and headed to the door. They walked to the transport together and Alex waved once Sierra was seated. She turned to walk to her car as the transport began to lift off. After another minute it was gone. Alex opened the door to her car and heard the unmistakable sound of fire. Her head snapped up and she saw that several of the houses on the street were being consumed by fire.

She saw movement in the air above Sierra's house and jumped when she realized a dragon was hovering in the air above it. It was terrifyingly beautiful; with Jade green scales and a dark maroon underbelly. The dragon spewed fire from its mouth that latched onto the house like napalm, and the flames began eating their way down the building; brick, wood, and stone. She hurriedly jumped in her car, an 88 Shelby Daytona, and cranked her up. She saw the dragon's head swivel toward her just as she pushed in the gas and released the clutch to speed out of the suburban neighborhood.

She was terrified, and the streets were starting to fill up with other panicked drivers, but she knew she had to lose the attention that she had inadvertently drawn to herself. *Bob and weave*, she thought to herself, and was amazed that she could still make a joke at that point. She made it to her rented house on the north side and roared down the gravel driveway, not caring that she was scattering gravel to each side and peppering the underside of her car with it. She made it into the house, sat down on her couch, and it felt like the walls were closing in on her. She felt she needed the slightly claustrophobic feeling to be able to process the happenings outside.

First things first, she thought to herself. Alex had a pretty clear idea of what she needed to do. Lying low wouldn't work well for her; putting her head in the sand had never been her style. She decided on two goals on which to focus. First, she was going to need some supplies. There was an out of the way mom and pop grocery store that very few people knew about a couple of miles up the road. She figured that might be the safest place away from all the traffic and looters that she guessed would be at the major stores. Second - find him. He knew what was going on and she was determined to find out what this was all about.

She grabbed a couple of empty duffel bags from the closet and her emergency backpack. A few months back she had purchased the backpack and survival items online. She hadn't really been thinking about danger and was online surfing when she landed on the site late at night. She had chalked it up to a tired paranoia purchase, but she never had gotten around to returning it. Well, she was grateful now. She grabbed one of the empty duffel bags and went to the pantry to pack what meager canned goods she had on hand.

She went to her bedroom and grabbed a couple of changes of clothes and personal items to stuff into the bag. She dressed in hiking gear and boots and grabbed a jacket. She packed the bags into the car and then stood for a moment as she said goodbye to her little rental house. She gave herself a moment and then bottled up those emotions and put them in a compartment in her head. She got in the car and drove to the grocery store. She saw flames past the tree line along the way where she knew homes and local businesses were located, and she hoped that everyone had gotten out of the buildings before the fires destroyed them.

When she arrived there was only one car in the parking lot. It looked like it always did, so she assumed no looters had come this way yet and she saw no flames near the store. She entered the store and walked toward the office where Edith and George, the older couple that owned the place, were always located. She rounded the doorway and came face to face with a shotgun. Her eyes got blurry for a second as she thought, *this might be it*. George immediately recognized her and quickly brought the barrel down, apologizing as he did so.

"George, calm down, Alex understands. Don't you, dear?"
Edith piped in.

"I take it y'all have been dealing with looters?" Alex asked while she tried to calm her racing heart. She looked around and saw the mess. At that George's face flushed with anger, "A man held a gun to my wife's head! We told him to take what he wanted and he did. He just left about ten minutes ago, and I went and got my shotgun just in case anyone else tried an asshole move like that." "I'm so sorry that happened to you. People panic in terrible ways. Are y'all hurt?" Alex asked.

"No, I'm just mad." Edith answered, "It was Nate Stuartson that held a gun to my head. He and some of his cronies trashed the place. We've known that man for years, and this is how he repaid that friendship? Sorry that you walked into the aftermath of that, dear."

"No, it's okay, I completely understand." Alex assured them, "Why haven't you gotten on a transport yet?"

"We're headed to the bomb shelter under my father's corn field. Crazy old coot built it during the bomb scare, but it looks like it'll come in handy now. I don't trust these "protected cities." Sounds a lot like concentration camps to me," George stubbornly replied.
"We're just here to pack up some food ourselves, and to gather some mementos and such from the office," Edith added.
"You're welcome to grab what you need and come with us, child," George offered.

"Thank you for the offer. I think I will grab some supplies. I've got to figure out what's going on, though. I think I know someone to ask, so I'm going to find him. I'll find you once I know more," Alex answered.

George and Edith shared a quick look and Edith nodded her head once. "Here," George said as he went to the desk and opened a drawer. "Take this with you for protection, girl," he handed her a silver 9mm handgun. "Stay safe," Edith added.

"I will, and you two as well. Thank you," Alex replied. She stuck the gun into her waistband at the small of her back and waved as she picked up her bag. She heard Edith and George's old Ford crank up and take off shortly after. She quickly grabbed some food that wouldn't spoil quickly and stuffed it into her bag along with bottled waters, a first aid kit, and some necessary toiletry items.

She went back out to the car and paused as she was putting her supplies in. She looked to the doors of the supermarket and saw a shadow push open the door and disappear. Her heart rate sped up and she kept her eyes moving looking for any sign of movement. Goosebumps broke out on her arms and she knew she was being watched. She quickly jumped in the driver's seat and screeched out of the parking lot.

She calmed herself as best she could and headed to Johnson's hunting lodge; she feared she would need more than a fifteen shot handgun in the coming days. The feeling of being watched went away once she was out of sight of the grocery store. There were several cars in the parking lot when she arrived. She approached the door very carefully. She pulled her handgun out as she neared the doors, fearful that someone had decided to stand at the door to try to claim the building for themselves.

She saw that her fears were unfounded when she pushed through the doors. It was loud, people were yelling at each other, but once she made out the words, she almost laughed out loud in relief. These good ole' boys were telling newcomers which weapons to go for, and how they had always known either civil war or the apocalypse would come one of these days.

A couple of the guys that worked there recognized Alex and yelled hello. One of them turned around to the selection of bows behind them and grabbed one down. "Guess you can have that compound bow you've been drooling over for the past three months," he said as he passed it over. It was true; she came out to Johnson's twice a week to practice with their hunting bows, and had been trying to save up for the bow now in her hands. "Thanks, Gene, I was hoping it would still be here."

"Not a problem, sugar, we knew we'd see ya so we held on to it. We had one guy try to loot here when the fires started, so we decided to keep it nice and friendly in here so nobody would get hurt. Just take what you need and stay safe out there." And then he was off to help another "customer."

Alex grabbed a couple of quivers and a ton of arrows and slid them into her bag. She then grabbed a couple of hunting knives with holsters, one for each arm, and some extra clips with 9mm rounds. On her way out the door she yelled to the guys behind the counter to stay safe.

Alex needed a quiet space for the next part of her journey so she headed to the park just down the road. She pulled in at the gate to Flat Rock Park and parked a few feet in. There was nobody else around so she pulled out all of her supplies and did a quick inventory. She grabbed a can of corn and opened it with the can opener she had just barely managed to remember to grab from her home. She scarfed it down quickly and then began packing everything back up in as close to an organized fashion as possible. Then she used some of the bungee cord from her emergency backpack to tie all the bags together and make it into a pack that she could carry all together.

She slid the straps over her shoulders and stood up. The pack was heavy but she could carry it with no problem. *Good thing I've kept up with my workouts*, she thought to herself. She walked to the tallest rock and climbed on top of it. She set her pack down and then sat down with her legs crossed and her eyes closed. She focused on the man that she had seen on the television until she could see every detail in his face. *Handsome,* she thought, then buried it quickly so that she wouldn't lose her concentration. She sent her awareness out into the world while keeping his face in her mind's eye. Farther and farther she sent her awareness until she felt what she could only describe as a ping on her mental radar. She focused on that ping and got a general direction to his location.

She opened her eyes, grabbed her pack, and headed back to her car. From before she could even remember, Alex had always had a knack for finding things and reading people's intentions. She had always kept these abilities to herself because she knew how people would react to anything different. She had trusted her instincts and kept her "gifts" to herself, but she had a strong feeling that she would need to explore them further very soon.

She got in the car and headed north. The interstate system was still in place, so she drove onto I-85 toward Atlanta. She got just south of Fairburn and pulled into what used to be a rest stop but had turned into an open clearing overgrown with wildflowers. North from that point the interstate had disappeared. It looked like a forest had grown where the road had been just hours earlier. She drove her car through the clearing and parked just inside the tree line. She grabbed all her gear and climbed out of the car. *This one might hurt a bit,* she thought to herself. She turned back to her beloved car and silently thanked it for its service. Then she bottled up her regret at leaving it and marched on.

Chapter Two: The Start of a Journey

It was eerie hiking through the forest where there had been a thriving city just the day before. She hadn't seen anyone since she left the highway. She had been walking for almost six hours judging by the sun's lowering position in the sky. She figured she had to be close to Atlanta. She had felt tremors in the ground for the last few hours and watched as what appeared to be skyscrapers rose above the tree line in the distance, almost as if they were growing up from the earth itself.

Alex finally reached the edge of the forest just as it began to get darker. Where the tree line ended, Alex could see a beautiful, glittering city but it looked nothing like the confusing streets and sections of Atlanta. The towers that had been visible for the last hour of her hike were now almost directly in front of her and they were breathtaking. Gems of all types and sizes adorned each building, as though the earth had wanted to show off its hidden beauty. There were veins of gold and silver that ran along the walls of the buildings, as though the building might bleed riches if it were harmed.

She shook herself free of the awe that the towers inspired and sat down on a boulder just inside the tree line. She pulled a protein bar and a can of boiled peanuts out of her pack and made a quick meal of them. She pulled up her inner radar and kept it focused on the man that she was searching for. She sent it out and it pinged almost immediately. He was no more than a few blocks away from her position. She thought about how best to approach the man and decided that going to see him before she had a safe place to run to, if need be, would be very stupid. She would have to find him in the morning, after she found a place to lay low.

She put on her pack and took in the view and sounds in front of her. She didn't see or hear anything to suggest that there were people here. She waited a few more minutes, then took off for the nearest tower, sticking as close to the shadows as possible. She kept tight to the building until she got to the doorway where she checked for signs of an alarm system. She crept through the doorway, mentally crossing her fingers that there would be no shriek of an alarm system firing up. She stood in the shadowed foyer and strained her ears for any sound of movement. She heard nothing but she did feel something. As soon as she crossed the threshold she felt the beginnings of an amazing sense of peace, and now it seemed to bleed into her pores so that she felt light on her feet. She closed her eyes and lifted her face to the ceiling with a smile on her face.

Somewhere in the back of her mind a flashing strobe of red started going off. It was interfering with her sense of peace and safety; she tried to toss it out of her head, but it stubbornly refused to stop. She snapped back to reality with an almost audible pop and darted into the shadows underneath what appeared to be a receptionist's desk. There was still nothing to suggest that she was not alone after several minutes, and she decided it was something about the building that had done that to her. The air smelled so much of earth, honeysuckle, and newly cut grass that it seemed to be taking her back to childhood summers spent playing with neighborhood kids. She felt a tugging in her mind that was trying to take her farther into those memories.

She pictured the man that she was here to find. She focused on his face and the strength of his presence. Then she drew on that strength. She felt an almost audible pop separate her from the draw, but she also felt his awareness swing toward her. He didn't seem to be able to pinpoint her like she was able to pinpoint him, so she felt reasonably safe for the moment. At least she was once again herself and was no longer fighting off the paralyzing effects of the environment around her.

Alex was still alone, but she knew that could change in an instant. She stood and looked around the foyer. To the left and right of the receptionist desk were grand, sweeping staircases that led up to the next floor. She looked toward the doorway and saw elevators on either side of the short walk from the doors to the desk. She didn't know if the structure had power so she took the stairs to the right of the desk up to the next floor and entered a hallway with several doors on each side.

Hotel Earth, she thought to herself as she ran her hand down one of the walls. They were made of some kind of mud, wood, and metal mesh. She pushed against the wall and felt it push back. It seemed to equalize itself against the amount of pressure that was exerted against it. *Pretty cool*, she thought. She entered a random door on the left and closed it behind her. She reached for a lock that wasn't there and then stood back as the wall and the door seamlessly grew together. She guessed that would have to do and turned to face the room she had entered. It was perfectly suited to her needs, and she watched as the windows were quickly covered by growing ivy. Once it seemed impossible for light to escape the room, small globes of light sparked to life and illuminated the room with slightly flickering light, like candle light.

Alex walked down two steps into a small living room and realized that everything in there was completely green. Not the color, although there was a lot of that, more like the movement that had recently dominated the world that was meant to preserve the earth. Everything was made by some form of the earth or by something connected to it. The coffee table and side tables looked like they had actually grown from the floor into their current shapes.

She walked over to the chair in the room and pressed down on the seat. It, and the sofa, were full of what felt like sand. It was soft but still had the right amount of firmness so that she wouldn't sink into it and never be able to emerge. The covering felt like the soft, suede feel of the underbellies of magnolia leaves.

She looked up at the globe of light above her. It appeared to be a small flame in a weird little bubble, and when she touched it the bubble gave a little, then bounced back to its proper shape when she removed her finger. She then rounded the sofa and went through the door into the bedroom. The bed was made in the same fashion as the chair and sofa, with a soft comforter on top. Alex couldn't tell what was inside the fabric so she sliced a small line with one of her knives. Dandelion fluffs, she realized. Millions of the weightless seeds. She put the comforter down and walked to the doorway beside the bed. She entered the connected bathroom and stopped in pure awe.

The bathroom was like a rainforest. It was a tropical paradise. She barely noticed the toilet and sink made of wood and that same mesh from the walls as she stepped toward the beautiful shower. There was no glass to hide behind here, instead there were large, interwoven leaves that somehow locked together so that water would stay within the structure. The handles for the water were made of jewels, and she looked back and noticed the same thing on the sink. Rubies had fused together on one handle. She assumed the ruby red indicated the hot water since the other handle was made of fused blue diamonds.

She turned both of the shower handles and gasped. One small side of the large shower remained dry, on the opposite side was a small waterfall from an outcropping of rock close to the ceiling, and in between both, the water fell from the ceiling like a gentle rain. What caught her breath the most was when the water hit the floor it was immediately absorbed into it, traveled up the back of the structure, and passed through what appeared to be a built-in individual filtration system. From there, it again became the water falling from the ceiling in a self-renewing cycle.

How freaking cool, she thought. She set her pack down and undressed in order to try it out. She stepped inside and almost died from pleasure. After soaping up and rinsing down she closed her eyes and just basked in the enjoyment and peace of the shower. When she began thinking of how peaceful and at one with the earth she felt, her inner alarm shouted at her again. She thought of the man she was searching for and again felt that odd mental pull as she snapped back to reality. She shut off the water and stepped out.

As her weight settled onto the soft rug outside of the shower, a strong, warm breeze came straight through the walls. She was dry in minutes. She grabbed a change of clothes from her pack and put them on. She then pulled a rope from her emergency pack and strung it across the room. She washed her hiking clothes in the sink and hung them up. She placed her weight on the rug again and that same warm current swept through the room and began drying her clothing. She left her hiking boots on the rug to keep the breeze moving over the clothes. She grabbed her sleeping bag and walked into the bedroom.

Alex couldn't chance sleeping on the bed for fear that she might get too comfortable and not be able to hear her inner alarm warning her while she slept. She spread the bag out on the side of the bed out of sight of the doorway and zipped herself into it. She thought of how exposed she still was if anyone made it into the room, and she suddenly started sinking. She jumped up out of the sleeping bag and watched as it sank into a cushioned hole that was a little longer and wider than she was. Stairs grew out of the wall in the hole as she watched, and she cautiously stepped down them.

When she reached the bottom her head barely cleared the top of the hole. She sat down again in her sleeping bag and watched as an opaque veil slid into place above her head. The room above her appeared exactly as it did before and she had a feeling that while she could see through the veil above her, no one would be able to see through it from the opposite side.

She didn't know if it was some new technology or what, but she decided that deeper thoughts on it could wait until she woke up. She yawned and leaned back in her sleeping bag. The last thing she thought of before she fell asleep was his face.

...

Come on, he thought to himself. Finally, after what felt like ages, Raziel finished his question and answer session. "Everyone knows their next steps. If you need help you can always call to us for it. Be at peace." The angel then disappeared from sight and most of the people in the room let out a sigh of relief. Angels were scary sons of bitches but the sigh was because they were also the most micro-managing faction in their alliance. Granted, they had the gift of partial foresight and could recognize the choices needed to be made in order to achieve success in this endeavor, but they came across as more bossy than farseeing.

As Tristan stood to exit the meeting chamber, a random picture of Alexandria crossed his mind. He knew her name was Alexandria, Alex for short. She had Nordic features: silver blond hair and argent blue eyes. She had high cheekbones and a button nose. She smiled a lot. She was tall, 5'10" maybe 5'11" and was both lean and curvy.

His homework had revealed nothing about her birthplace or her childhood before the age of five when she showed up in kindergarten in this small town in Georgia. She had no parents or siblings and lived in the foster care system until she was eighteen years of age. From everything he could gather she had not been abused but had never stayed longer than a year or two with any of the foster families. Not the most loving childhood. He had been drawn to her but had known that there was too much about to happen to see what that meant.

He felt a small flutter in his mind, as though mental fingers were trying to probe into his thoughts. He threw his shields into place and tried to trap the mental fingers where they were. Whoever was trying to get in was too fast. He felt the painful shockwave that went through the other person's mental defenses as his shield grazed them.

He looked around but could see no one that showed the pain of such a mental burn. He made a mental note to look into his colleagues a bit more and exited the room. The doorway led onto a large balcony on the roof. There was no other way into the penthouse than the balcony. That way only those in the officers' ranks and above could get to the meeting room.

Tristan cleared his mind as the others began to exit onto the roof. Once all of the Draigkin officers had gathered on the balcony, Tristan stepped forward. "Gentlemen, thank you for your efforts today. You have done well, but there is much left for us to do. We now have our orders. Go and fulfill your duties for this night. Be sure to watch out for the innocents and protect them if you have cause while you are out. We may have dealt a blow that causes our enemies to pause and regroup, but they are by no means going to stay down.

"Keep your eyes open and stay on alert. There may be things that you do not know at play. Go with speed." With that, most of the Draigkin shook out their wings and took flight. Once they left the roof, their camouflage kicked in and Tristan could no longer see them. It was an ability that only the oldest of them had developed;

that's why they were Officers and Generals. They had the ability to remain unseen by the enemy in order to gain intel on enemy movement, and to flank the enemy during battle.

Tristan's personal Guard remained on the roof. It was a group of six of his best Officers with whom he had developed strong friendships over the years. They made their way over to him. "What was that all about?" Simeon asked. Simeon was the most straight-forward of the group. He got to the point quickly, and usually with little to no tact.

"Just a warning for us not to let our guard down," Tristan answered. "We are close to being fully prepared for what is coming at us, but we are not there yet. It is important to still remain cautious, and to not get cocky during this enterprise."

"You worry a lot old man," Brandon laughed. Brandon was the most reckless of his Officers, but he was his Second-in-Command. There was no one that Tristan trusted more. At that moment, Tristan felt a strong sapping of his strength.

It was just a small amount that was taken, not enough to weaken him, but the fact that anyone could draw it from him was nearly impossible to comprehend. He sent his awareness out in search of the cause but could not pinpoint it. His Guards had snapped to alert as they had apparently, accurately, read what had happened.

"What the hell just happened, boss?!" Christian asked incredulously. "That shouldn't be possible."

"I know. It didn't feel malevolent, though, strange is it sounds," Tristan answered.

Brandon said, "I feel like there's something that we're missing. Me and the guys have been feeling some tension recently. I know this part is supposed to be a breeze, but there's something wrong."

"I know," Tristan said quietly. "There was a lower level demon trying to transport into the lobby here before the protections kicked in and banished him back to Mirgrash. Just after the meeting I felt someone try to break through my mental shields. I damaged them when I locked my thoughts, but I saw nothing that gave away who it was."

Brandon was straight to the point, "We have a spy."

"So it would seem," Tristan agreed. "I need you all on this. Find the spy as quickly as you can. Once the next step begins, we become a lot more vulnerable to attack before the window closes. We have to get the mortals in place and protected before the war begins. Scan everyone else. If you find a hint of something off about anyone, Draigkin, Angel, whatever, bring your suspicions to me. We'll meet here tomorrow evening while the patrols go out."

He clapped Brandon on the shoulder and Brandon did the same. "Happy hunting," Tristan said very seriously. He nodded to the rest of his Guard and they spread their wings and took off. They followed him to his balcony and then disappeared into the night as they started their search.

...

Tristan awoke before dawn. After a quick shower he quickly dried and put on a pair of combat pants. He went to his bedroom and began his morning ritual. He assembled his weapons on the bed and lined them up side by side. He put on a t-shirt that was tight enough to not get in the way but not so tight that it gave away the placement of his weapons.

He clipped a couple of combat knives along his belt and in his pocket. He then sheathed two double bladed short swords and put them in personalized holders on his back. The grips peeked over his shoulders for an easier draw and barely showed over the leather jacket he threw on. He then camouflaged his Focus, the source for his own magic, into the tattoo of an eagle on his chest. He had several tattoos so that his Focus couldn't be distinguished easily. He had completed this ritual every morning for a very long time, so it took only a few moments for him to get ready. He walked out onto the balcony. His wings arced up through twin holes in the back of his jacket and he jumped high into the sky with his wings flared to catch the wind. He could feel the air currents flowing around the sensitive leather-like appendages as he made sure he was invisible to any possible innocents below. Officers and Generals not only had the ability to hide in plain sight, they were also able to alter their form to their will. The lower level dragons could only carry the form of a human or their dragon.

He loved flying, and he basked in the freedom it brought for a few minutes. His responsibilities were weighing heavily on him lately, and he felt as though he would suffocate if not for the small moments that he could spare to take flight. Tristan was restless. He decided to head over to the Forest Tower to make sure that everything was to his specifications.

He banked to the left to head there and decided to land at the doors so that he could make sure everything looked in place from the doors all the way to the living areas. He walked through and bypassed the elevators on both sides. He was smacked in the face with the building's defenses. They were unusually high and had he been a normal mortal he wouldn't have been able to shake off the wave of tranquility. He tamped down the building's defenses. It wouldn't do to have the humans stopped dead in their tracks in the doorway from the overwhelming feelings the defenses engendered.

He let the defenses lightly seep through the walls instead of in a pounding waterfall and headed to the stairs on the left side of the receptionist's desk. At the top he strode into the conference room that took up the entire left wing of the first floor. He thought about exactly how he wanted the room to look and kept focused on that image while the room shifted until everything was in the correct place.

A marble podium had grown onto a stage that looked as if the top of a tree had been filed off and the roots had been exposed. The same mesh from the walls covered the top of the podium in a flat surface. Chairs of oak, ash and cedar had grown out of the floor on both the stage facing out and on the lower floor facing the stage. The wall behind the stage had become almost opaque so that the room was flooded with natural light.

The plan for the newly reshaped cities, hearth cities as it had been decided to call them, was to create new governments and laws for each based on the needs and precautions of each individual hearth city. *True Democracy,* he thought to himself. There would be a conglomerate of leaders that were chosen by the people in the community. They would be elected by the people, they would vote on decisions that affected their community, and they would live in that same community so that they were held accountable for their choices, and would actually know the people they served. It would take time, but it would work.

Chapter Three: Quest for Truth

Alex shot upright in bed and tried to concentrate on what had woken her. She cautiously crawled out of the sleeping bag and quietly walked up the steps to the floor above her. It was still quiet in the apartment. Something had woken her though. She rolled up her bedroll and took it to the bathroom. She then repacked the rope and clothing that she had left in there. She double checked that her weapons and ammo were still there and then placed her handgun into the waist of her jeans, strapped her bow and quiver along her back, and clipped the knives in their holsters to the belt around her hips.

She brushed her teeth and hair and then strapped her makeshift pack back on, careful to make sure that she could still reach her weapons. She went to the door, willed it to open just a crack and was surprised when it did just that.

The hallway was clear and quiet, so she stepped out slowly. She walked to the stairway and peeked over the edge. The lobby was empty; however, she heard noises coming from the opposite wing. Before she went to check it out, she sent her mental radar out to search for the man she needed to find. She was very surprised when it pinged so quickly. It seemed the man was in the building with her. She silently hurried to the other side of the staircase. She peeked around the threshold and saw the room shifting just like her bedroom had last night. She also saw the man she was searching for standing near the windows, apparently lost in thought.

As natural light poured into the room, she decided on a direct approach. She took a step inside and cleared her throat. He turned quickly and surprise flashed over his features. "Alexandria! What are you doing here?" he said and took an involuntary step toward her.

"You seem to be the man with all the answers, so I hunted you down," she answered. The man stopped himself from stepping forward again and his eyes seemed to shift. She would swear they were yellow, like a hawk's eyes, but she knew from seeing him on television that they were blue. Her confusion showed on her face; she knew her face expressed her every emotion. He seemed absolutely taken aback.

Alex blinked and he was there, right in front of her with barely a couple of inches between them. He had just crossed approximately two football fields in the time it took her to blink, and his eyes were a rapid kaleidoscope of color as he peered down into her own. Alex was freaked out and jumped several feet back from him dropping into a fighting stance that she had learned in the handful of Krav Maga classes that she had actually attended. *Wish I had gone to more,* she ruefully thought.

He held his hands up in front of his chest with his fingers spread wide in the classic "I mean you no harm" gesture. "I'm sorry if I frightened you," he began, "I just didn't...," he seemed to be at a loss for words as he trailed off. Comprehension dawned on his features, and his eyes did that weird color switch and became a clear mint color. "You don't know!" he exclaimed, and then he seemed confused again.

"Look, buddy, I don't know what your issue is, but you're seriously creeping me out." At that moment she heard the sounds of people walking into the building. She heard masculine laughter. She watched as she saw genuine fear cross his features.

"No! You can't be here right now," he quietly exclaimed. He tried to grab her forearm. She quickly shifted out of his reach.

"I'm not going anywhere until I know what is going on," she fiercely whispered back. Perhaps it was the fear that she had seen that made her answer more quietly than she would have normally.

He sighed and said, "That's a really long conversation that we don't have time for right now. I need to get you somewhere safer."

"I've got all the time in the world right now," she shot back. She knew that he could see the intensity written all over her face because he ran his fingers through his hair in an agitated way.

"Okay, we do need to talk, but I can't let you be seen, not here and not yet. Please just go stand in that corner, just until this part is over. Then we'll have a long conversation. I give you my word," he pleaded. She listened to her instincts, and they were telling her to trust him. She nodded but added, "I'll hold you to that." Then she turned and walked to the corner as the sound of voices and laughter got closer.

As Alex grew closer, leaves parted in a small nook of the corner and then closed around her so that the corner appeared exactly as it had before she was hidden. She guessed he was being polite because he had made sure that the leaves in front of her face kept her hidden but also allowed her to see what was going on in the room.

He seemed to be looking at her eyes through a two-way mirror, near but not quite on target. Some emotion flickered over his features that she couldn't place, but then he turned and faced the doorway just before a large group of men entered.

Very large, she thought to herself, not only in numbers but in presence and figure as well. They seemed larger than life, and she realized that while she hadn't noticed it before, it had been the same with the man that she had been searching for as well. There were well over two hundred men in the room now; it felt like the room couldn't hold any more, but there was still plenty of space in the room.

They all seemed to defer to the man as though he were a leader. She couldn't make out very much that was spoken; there were too many voices. Everyone began making their way to the seats, and her mystery man made his way toward the front podium. *Damn,* she thought, *I could have at least asked for his name, I do have manners... sometimes.*

The next fifteen to twenty minutes were spent basically going over assignments as they prepared for the influx of people about to arrive in the city. Some people were supposed to be tour guides. Quite a few of them were apparently counselors who would help calm people, and others were put on guard duties. *Pretty boring meeting,* Alex thought.

No one seemed to be going anywhere for the time being and they were all still focused on preparations. She wasn't going to learn anything useful here, and she wanted to go back to the room that she had claimed the night before. She waited a moment more until she was sure that she wouldn't be seen, then concentrated on parting the leaves around her. As soon as she thought it, it was done. She kept her eyes on the crowd and quickly walked the few feet to the door and out. She was sure she hadn't been seen, and she continued on to her room on the opposite wing.

She had just closed the door behind her when she heard a knock. The knock didn't come from the door, though. It was inside her head. She turned to the door and pictured a peephole. Once it appeared, she peered through it, but no one was there. The mental knocking came again. Alex really didn't know what to do, so she went with her best guess.

She pictured a door in her mind and sent a hesitant mental call out, *Who's there?* She winced as her words came out more as a shout. She heard her mystery man's voice on the outside, as if from a very long distance away. *It's me, where did you go? Are you okay?* He sounded concerned for her. *I'm fine*, she mentally whispered this time. *I can't hear you*, he called back.

Well, crap, she thought to herself. She focused and mentally pictured herself in front of the door in her mind. Her mental image reached for the door handle, and she heard the sound of many locks disengaging as she turned the handle and opened the door. There an image of him stood, his changeling eyes meeting her own. Again his eyes seemed to change colors a few times until they landed on an anxious, tangerine color.

Sorry, this is really weird, and I can't figure out what volume I should be thinking at, she thought to him in a barely-there whisper. One corner of his mouth turned up, and his eyes became a soft, almost amused teal. *I understand,* he thought to her, *It takes a minute or two to modulate your tone the first time you speak telepathically, but then you'll have the hang of it. If it helps, picture a room around you and you'll think in a level equal to the space*

42

around you almost naturally. At that she looked around and realized that her voice had been echoing from a vast emptiness.

She blushed just a little and thought to him, *Now I'm embarrassed. I promise I'm not empty headed,* she joked self-deprecatingly. She began forming a room in her head. What appeared was surprising. The room was about the size of a living room and had two wing chairs with a table in between. What was surprising were the things that were there that she hadn't thought about. The walls of the room were spaced every few feet with locked steel doors.

On the contrary, he thought to her, *this is highly interesting. Your apparent ability to lock all thoughts away and shield them from view is probably the most talented of anyone that I've ever communicated with in this way. Did you imagine these shields into place?*

No, I just tried to imagine a room, she thought back and was surprised to find that the words had come across at the right volume level. He smiled that lopsided grin again, and she realized that her surprise must have been written all over her face.

His mental image faltered for a minute and blurred. When his image came back into focus she asked him about it. *Sorry,* he answered, *we're finishing up the meeting and I'm answering questions.*

How can you split your concentration like that? I'm crouched down

43

beside a doorway because I'm scared to open my eyes and ruin my concentration here, she gestured at the room.

It just takes a little practice, he answered.

Alex held out her hand for a shake. *I'm Alex,* she said. He laughed out loud and shook her hand. *I'm Tristan,* he said. *I forgot for a moment that we haven't officially met.* She gestured to a chair and invited him in. *If I'm going to let you in, I figured it was a good idea to know your name.*

He shook his head and took a step back from the door. *I can't come in right now,* he said. *I need to finish here.*

But I have so many questions left, she thought anxiously.

I will answer them to the best of my ability, he thought. *I'll find you after my men and I are done here. Where are you?*

Still in the building, she thought back. *Opposite wing from the room you're in. Fifth door on the left.*

Okay, I'll see you after, he said, and then he disappeared from her mind. Alex opened her eyes and stood from her crouched position by the door. She walked into the living room and sat on the sofa. Her mind was still racing from all that she had learned today, so she allowed her mind to vent its confusion so she could relax. She thought about everything that had happened that brought her to this moment in order to get her questions sorted in her mind. She let her mind wander for a little while, jumping from random thought to random thought as she relaxed into the cushions.

She was in that in-between place just before sleep overwhelmed her when she felt a weird disturbance in the air. She jumped to her feet and looked cautiously around her. There was a blurring in the space near the kitchen doorway.

Alex instinctively knew that this was a very bad thing. She circled around the sofa until she was able to retreat to the bedroom doorway. She pulled her bow off of her back and an arrow out of her quiver. She notched the arrow just as something materialized out of the blur. It was grotesque. It looked like a human-sized cockroach that had learned to stand on two legs and was almost as tall as Alex. Its face was more like a cobra head with its flared neck flaps, and its eyes were black, no visible white, and eerily empty. As if there was no soul behind those eyes, just evil.

In the split second it took for these thoughts to form she loosed an arrow at its heart. The arrow hit its mark, but the creature didn't go down. It turned those evil eyes on her and flared its wings. It flew to the ceiling and began scrambling to her. The click of its legs on the ceiling tiles was loud, and Alex notched another arrow. She waited for it to look at her again, then shot it through one of its evil little eyes. There was a horrible screeching and clicking sound, and then it was gone with nothing but a large spot of gray ash on the ceiling: an arrow stuck where it had pierced through the thing. There was a weird smell in the air, but Alex barely noticed.

She just sat down with her bow in her lap and stared at the spot on the ceiling. She felt kind of shocked, her heart was racing, and her appendages had gone numb. *It wasn't every day that you ran into a hundred pound cockroach with a snake's head*, she thought to herself almost hysterically. Then the thought came into her head, *what if there are more coming?*

While her mind started thinking gibberish, she lifted her hand from her lap, and slapped herself as hard as she could. Her brain stopped rambling, and she hung on to the stinging pain in her cheek to keep herself grounded in the here and now.

She heard a knock at the door, and her bow was up and an arrow notched before she even thought about it. She sent her mental radar out and it pinged on Tristan standing on the other side of the door. She re-secured the bow on her back and went to open the door. "Déjà vu", she said and thought, *well, at least my sense of humor is working.* He started to smile then frowned as he saw what she guessed was a red imprint of her hand on her face. His eyes flashed an inhuman red and he growled, literally growled, low in his throat, "Who did this to you?"

She stepped back and put her hand on her bow, "Me, actually," she said. He quickly doused the flames in his eyes and lowered them.

46

"My apologies. I did not mean to frighten you. I am concerned, why would you...?" His head came up quickly and his eyes flared bright red again as they surveyed the room. His nostrils flared, and quicker than she could blink, he was standing in front of her, two swords drawn and facing the room; his body tensed for a fight.

"Ceiling," she said drily. He stared up at the ash for a second, and then he sheathed his swords and turned back to her. His eyes were the yellow predator eyes of a bird of prey. They were a little disturbing as he looked at her.

"Can you change those?" She gestured at his eyes.

"I'm sorry, I can't. You are one of very few people who can see what I'm feeling through my eyes. I do not know how they appear to you right now."

"Like hawk eyes," she said. "I feel like you're sizing me up as prey."

"On the contrary," he replied, "I am sizing you up as a predator. Tell me what happened," he paused a moment and seemed to realize that came out as a command. "If you would... please," he corrected.

Alex explained everything, even down to her almost-lost-it there moment as he wanted to know what happened to her face. His eyes changed to what came across as a relieved navy color. "Very impressive," he said. "You destroyed a low-level demon on your own and with no injuries, besides the self-inflicted slap. I am glad you're okay. You did well." She felt her cheeks warm a little at the praise, so she deflected his attention,

"Now I have a ton of questions," she said. He nodded in acknowledgement of the change in subject and went to the sofa to sit down. "You know the main parts now, but you can ask me your questions. I will answer all that I can," he said. This statement caused a new question, and she asked, "All that you can. Does that mean that there may be things that you aren't able or..." she watched his face for a reaction, "aren't allowed to?" There, a flicker in his eyes almost too quick to see, and she knew she had it right. He nodded in a touché gesture with a little smile.

"You are very smart, and, yes, there are things that I am unable to tell you as of now, but in the future I will be able to. I will not lie to you, I promise you that." He spoke earnestly and she believed him, but she couldn't let him know that. She said, "My trust has to be earned."

She sat down in the chair across from him. "Well my first question was who are the enemies coming for us, but I guess that cockroach thing answered that one."

"Somewhat," he answered. "That is one type of the enemies coming after us. The details to the public were vague for a reason.

48

Most people are not yet mentally prepared to accept us, let alone our enemies. What you killed was a Nefret demon. It thrives on hate and disgust, which is why it usually appears in a form of what the person it appears to has an aversion to." She absorbed this, then asked, "What do you mean by 'us'?"

"The world is not as black and white as most people believe. They have now seen some evidence of that with the video of a sky battle. There are beings that exist in the gray shadows of the world. These people are not human, and they exist on either side of the moral line. Those two sides are making a play for the earth right now.

"One side is trying to turn the earth into its hunting grounds. The other side, my side, is fighting to protect the human population of earth. The Draigkin have been protecting the earth's inhabitants since before most people could comprehend. We have an alliance with the angels in an effort to continue in this vein. There are other groups in our alliance, the shapeshifter clans, the light fey, and others that I cannot speak of yet.

The demons have teamed up with vampires, warlocks, the dark fey and others. We dealt a blow in the last battle that gave us a very small window of time to set up protections for the civilians. Our enemies don't care about collateral damage."

Alex sat in silence for a moment as she mulled over his words. She was not as shocked as she felt she would have been as she dealt with something that was very far out of her normal scope. She had always felt that there was more going on in the world than what she could see, and now she had her proof. When she looked at him again he was patiently waiting for her to finish processing what he had told her.

"Okay," she began, "I'm with you for the most part. Demons, vampires, etcetera, bad, got it. Makes sense. Angels, good, but what was that word again? What does it mean?"

"Draigkin," he answered. "It is what I am, and what my species collectively is called; it means dragon." He stopped and waited for her reaction.

She immediately asked, "Aren't dragons bad, though? The mythology on them is all about sacrificing virgins to them and knights trying to kill them on their quests for glory." He snorted out a little laugh.

"I hate that misconception. Dragons have always been protectors. The knights and virgins myths are actually intertwined. In the Dark and Middle ages women were possessions, not people in the eyes of men or laws. They were not allowed to speak in the presence of men and were not raised to be able to think for themselves or form opinions. The virgin daughters of a family were sent to the dragons in their region to be protected until the terms of their sale into marriage were negotiated.

"In those days a common way for the future groom to gain the upper hand in negotiations was to seduce or rape the female in question. While the girls were in the care of their dragon protectors, we began encouraging their creativity. We taught them how to be more independent and how to develop their own opinions. When they returned to their families, they began exerting their new found independence.

"Soon after that the men of the world began to hunt us. They were not happy about women learning that they could have power. We had to go underground. It was an unstoppable force by that point. Women were teaching their daughters how to think for themselves after that. The Renaissance began shortly after, the age of beauty and creativity."

Alex sat back in her chair and thought that over. "Wow. I guess all I have to say is Thank you."

He looked a little surprised at that, "For what?"

"Well, if dragons are to blame for women developing independence in the world, then I owe my life and freedom to you all. So thank you." His eyes flashed to a vibrant bright blue that she thought might be gratitude. She continued, "Okay, so Dragons, sorry Draigkin, and Angels are allies. How did that develop?"

"It began a very long time ago. The first dragon was created with all the animals in those first seven days along with Adam and Eve. You know the story, right?" she nodded, and he continued, "Well, most people know the version of the story where a serpent handed Eve the fruit from the tree of knowledge. That is slightly different from what actually occurred. My grandfather was the one who handed her the fruit." At this her eyes got really big, and she finally showed a little bit of shock.

"Don't judge him too harshly, though. Lucifer told him to do it, but most people forget that Lucifer was an angel before he fell. So when Lucifer gave my grandfather that command, he thought he was doing the right thing. The story claims that he was then forced to crawl on his belly but that was just a metaphor. God clipped his wings, but because he knew my grandfather's heart was in the right place and what had really happened, He allowed him the ability to live out his life with the ability to look like a man.

"That way he would not be killed for being the so called reason for Adam and Eve being thrown out of the garden, and he was able to begin the calling that God had given him. The dragon had been created to be a protector for God's creation, so once the humans were cast out into the world, it was even more imperative that they be watched over. So my grandfather began the Alliance. He started with the angels and has spent his life growing the factions that have pledged to protect the human race."

Alex was stunned. All of this was a bit overwhelming for her, but she had to ask, "So the dragons are now just men? And 'has spent'... does that mean your grandfather is still alive?" the last was said in serious disbelief.

"Alive and well, if a bit ornery and set in his ways," Tristan joked. "As to the other, no, the Draigkin are still dragons; I guess you could think of us as shapeshifters, in a way. We wear our human form to hide our true form so that we don't unnecessarily alarm the mortals. My grandfather's wings were clipped, but the rest of our species are as we were created in the beginning, just with an ability to blend in."

"I'm sorry," Alex said, "I just can't get over... How old is your grandfather? I mean... that's... how? And how does he possibly have a young grandson? I mean you're what... 29 or 30?"

Tristan's eyes flashed to a chagrined dark brown, "Not exactly. My grandfather's age is kind of difficult to pin down. You know how supposedly God sees time differently than man? Well, it's kind of the same for the Draigkin. While they were protected in the garden, millions of years went by. That's how there are dinosaur fossils and the theory of evolution. Yes, all of those theories are true, along with creationism, because there were other people already in the world when Adam and Eve were banished to it. That's how their sons were able to find wives and procreate. But for my grandfather, that was just a heartbeat of time.

"The mortals were thrust into the slower time stream when they left the garden but my grandfather remained in that time stream, and so have the Draigkin that came after him. So a year in mortal time could be a hundred years in our time, or just a heartbeat, but we can step into the human time stream when needed. Like we are doing now. So there is no clear answer to how old he is. As for me, I am quite a bit older than I appear in the mortal time stream, but I am in fact thirty years old in my time stream."

"Time out!" Alex said as she put her hands up in the air. "I think I need a little time to process some of this. I can't take any more revelations just yet."

"I'm sorry, but there are things that you must know." His face was very serious. Alex got up and paced to the windows, then spun back around to face him. "Okay, but I need a little space for a minute. Can you give me that?"

"As you wish. I'll be right outside when you are ready," Tristan answered. He stood and bowed slightly to her, then walked to the door. Her whole body went ice cold and chills raced down her neck and spine. *No!* her inner alarm screamed just as she reached for the large hunting knife on her hip, pulled it back, and then released it spinning through the air, between one blink and the next.

Just before the knife would have slammed into Tristan, a man materialized directly behind him and it instead collided with that man's spine. It made a sickening sound of metal on bone as the long knife scratched through. The man crumbled to the ground as

Tristan spun, both swords slashing through air where the man had been barely a second before. His eyes were an inhuman, fiery red as they flicked up to meet her shocked ones. Black flickers began to overtake her vision. Then the lights went out and she fell to the floor.

...

He felt the telltale chills on the back of his neck warning of an impending attack from behind. In one inhale he pulled his swords from their sheaths, turned and sliced through... air. He saw the crumpled body on the floor with what appeared to be a severed spine from the knife now sticking through where his spinal cord should have been. He checked to see that Alex was okay.

Alex was standing behind the couch, arm still held straight out from her body in perfect throwing form. Her fingers curled in as the strength left her arm and it fell to her side. His eyes met hers. He knew that his had to be bright with fiery adrenaline, but he was surprised at the silver shining back at him from hers. She shook once, then her eyes closed and she began falling. He realized that she was feeling the backlash of killing a Neshriki demon, a dangerous concussion blast to the mind if you weren't prepared for it.

With a burst of inhuman speed he raced to her side and caught her before she slammed into the floor. His fingers curled around her upper arms and as soon as the bare skin of her shoulders met his fingertips a shot of electricity burned through him straight to his brain.

He understood so much more now. What finding a Misakin on earth meant to the war, and what it meant for him. He knew he had to protect her at any cost from the danger she would be facing very soon. Her life was about to become very complicated. He stood with her in his arms and walked towards the balcony of the room she had chosen. He looked at her face, relaxed in unconsciousness, and felt a fierce protective instinct roll through him.

It's for the best that she not experience flight for the first time while terrified and weak, he thought to himself. Then he launched himself into the air as his camouflage protected them both.

Chapter Four: What Lies Before

Alex was back in the room in her mind, curled up on one of the beige chairs that had been there before. She cried uncontrollably for a long while as she remembered killing that man, without a second thought. She had never believed that she would be capable of that kind of violence.

I need my best friend, she thought, and cried even harder as she realized that she had no idea where Sierra was. She thought of how frightened Sierra must be, and she began to pull herself together. Sierra had always been so fragile and such a gentle soul that Alex had learned to be strong for the both of them. Then it hit her that she had no idea how to get out of this room.

She stood from the chair while she tried to fully wake up. No go. She looked around the room trying to see an exit as she brushed the tears away. She shook her head as if that would push the emotion further away and focused on the doors lining the room.

She walked to the nearest one and ran her hand along the seam where it met the wall. She wasn't surprised when it slowly pushed itself open, but she was surprised at what lay on the other side of it. She saw herself walking down the halls of the middle school she had attended.

Her head was down as she walked towards the doors to make her escape for the day, but Alex knew that she was constantly scanning her surroundings. She hazily remembered this day. She remembered she had gotten home after school that day with blood on her shirt and had no idea how the blood stain got there. At the time, she assumed it was another nose bleed.

Her younger self passed through the doors and got halfway down the stairs before she was stopped. She remembered the sick ball of resentment in her stomach as the resident bully stepped in her path. Jessica was the most popular girl in school, and by far the prettiest with her gorgeous chestnut hair, perfect complexion, and piercing amber-colored eyes.

All Alex had ever wanted to do was blend in, and somehow that had offended Jessica. Alex tried to step around her, and Jessica grabbed her long hair in a tight fist, yanking her head back. "Hey, nerd, where do you think you're going? Off to read those stupid books of yours?"

Alex was suddenly her younger self again and seeing things from right in the action. She could hear her younger self's thoughts and could see through her eyes, but couldn't move. She felt young Alex's resentment rise up and switch a flip in her mind. Alex's young mind dove straight into Jessica's with the goal of revenge, carrying her older self along for the ride.

She could see everything, Jessica's fear that people would realize she couldn't read because the letters moved around and never looked like real words. *Dyslexia,* her mature mind filled in. She saw Jessica's every insecurity and saw the memories of Jessica's mother screaming at her, jealousy twisting her image into an angry mask. *Beauty fades! You're too stupid to live! You're worthless without your pretty face!*

She saw Jessica's fear that her mother was right. She saw every beating Jessica received, and she saw the pattern repeating in Jessica's future. Picking on other girls in the hope that she could bring the same misery that she felt every day to others, so that she wouldn't be so scared and alone. Alex's grown mind saw it all, and her heart broke for this poor, lost little girl.

Alex realized this is not what her younger mind saw. Young Alex saw every time Jessica had hurt her, and every image of Jessica attacking her, either verbally or physically. These memories became razorblades in Jessica's mind. They stabbed and cut jagged streaks all over this poor girl's psyche, doing who-knows-what damage.

Once young Alex was finished, she returned to her own mind. She calmly removed Jessica's hand from her hair and smirked as she walked away, wiping the blood that was dripping from her nose absentmindedly. She reached out to everyone that had been near them to remove the memory of her confrontation with Jessica as the blood continued to drip down her second-hand blouse. She didn't look back, and Alex felt the memory disappear from her younger mind as it was casually tossed into a dark closet and locked away.

Alex was herself again, staring into a now empty closet in her mind. She dropped to the floor, horrified by what she had seen in herself, and began to vomit. She remembered that everyone at school had been so confused when Jessica never returned. She had gone to an asylum. The rumor spread that she had gone crazy and tried to kill her mother and herself.

Tears began to slowly drop down her cheeks as she wiped her mouth, stood back up, and looked around the room again. There had to be at least twenty doors that now struck her as sinister. Did they all contain memories? *Oh God, are they all that evil?* She thought to herself.

She tried again to wake herself up even going as far as to pinch and bite herself on the arm with no results. She was stuck in this room in her mind, surrounded by everything she had ever hidden away from herself. She reached deep for that core of strength and courage that had taken her on her search for answers. She knew she had to open these memories in order to return to herself, whoever that may be.

She crossed to a door on the other side of the room. It appeared to be old and barely hanging on to its hinges. She put her hand up to reach for the door and noticed the slight tremors that ran through her hand before she placed it against the door. It opened onto a scene from a dream; a backdrop of silver mountains against a bright blue sky and flowers everywhere around her, in colors that no human had ever seen.

Alex was present in her two year old mind as she toddled between the rows of flowers. Her younger self was fascinated with a flying insect that had landed on the flower just ahead. It was similar to a cross between a butterfly and a tiny hummingbird, its wings were going so fast that they created a picture in the air as they moved. Her mature mind was ever watchful of anything she could see on the peripheral of her vision.

She saw an unnaturally beautiful woman smiling while watching Alex toddle about. She had wings arching up over her shoulders that were, from what she could see, the color of the clearest ocean, almost a silver blue. *Alexandria, be gentle,* she called toward Alex as she reached out to grab those pretty wings in front of her. The woman looked up at the sun, which was a muted orange and then began walking toward her.

Young Alex giggled and tried to dart away as the woman reached to pick her up, but the woman was prepared for the move and lifted her up in her arms. *It is time to return home, my love, time to see your friends. Don't you want to see Ryder?* she cajoled. Young Alex felt a strong compulsion to be in the air, so she reached out to touch the woman's wings where they lifted above her shoulders and asked, *Fly?*

It's only a moment's walk, but as you wish darling, she smiled back at her, *One day you will be able to fly yourself there,* she teased. She stretched out her wings. What she thought had been only one color was most definitely not monochromatic. They were similar to the butterfly hybrid Alex had been looking at in that they matched on either side, but they darkened from that silver blue at the top and every color in between into a twilight deep purple with intricate silver designs throughout. The woman lifted up in the air and spun Alex around before going toward a distant building just past a copse of trees that, for the moment, kept her from seeing any other inhabitants.

Just before they would have exited the trees, the woman came to an abrupt halt in the air. Older Alex watched as the woman's face froze in shock and saw through young Alex's eyes as the sky turned blood red. Two year-old Alex was not happy about the change, and she began to cry and wail. Older Alex felt dread curl up in her stomach. The woman clapped her free hand over Alex's mouth, and even young Alex recognized fear in the woman's face and quieted quickly.

It was too late, though. Giant footfalls began to shake the trees around them and the woman turned and raced back the way they had come from. They flew by the clearing at a blinding speed as those steps kept echoing through the air, faster now as though whoever created them was running.

They reached a small cave on the side of a cliff and the woman dodged inside. She placed Alex against the back wall of the cave and knelt down in front of her, her wings spread on the ground around her like the train of a wedding dress. The woman placed her fingertip to young Alex's forehead. Present day Alex felt a closet in young Alex's mind open for the first time.

My darling, I know once you remember this I will be long gone. I hope to shield you from the pain of what is about to happen. The Nephilim have finally found a way to enter Ganeska, the dimension of the crossbreeds, where we have lived for eons with our trusted guardians. The Nephilim are the giant children of Cain's poor daughters, who fell victim to the fallen Angels' lusts. We had hoped that they were wiped out in the flood, but there have been rumors for centuries that there were survivors.

They are jealous of the Misakin, the children of Angel and Immortal pairings. You are a Neraako, the only one of your kind, as your father and I were not blessed with a sibling for you before he was killed. You are my daughter. I am an Angel, and your father was a Draigkin. The Nephilim believe that God cursed them because of their fathers. God did curse them, but because of their own behavior. Not because of their fathers. They destroyed everything they came across and let their human side turn ugly and horrifying.

63

They were sent to Mirgrash, the hell dimension, and have been plotting to get into Ganeska ever since the first pairing of Angels with the creatures of old. I don't know who had the knowledge to allow them access. You need to find out when you are older and able. Trust only yourself now. She choked up a little as the tears began to stream down her cheeks. *I will always be with you, my darling girl. Do not let them corrupt you as they will most certainly attempt to do.*

Alex felt a strong persuasion settle deep into her bones in her younger self as her mother next spoke, *You must escape this place once you are able. You will not be anyone's pawn, you are strong. You are Neraako, and not even I know all that you are capable of. You will forget this place and everything in it until you are ready.* The giant pounding footfalls reached the edge of the cliff. *I love you so much,* her mother whispered before touching her finger to young Alex's forehead again. As young Alex's eyes began to close, present day Alex saw a giant, deformed hand reach into the cliff and yank her mother out by her beautiful wings.

Alex came back to herself curled up in the fetal position in front of the door. She lost time as she allowed herself to grieve for the mother that she had never gotten to know. When she was able to pick herself up again, she felt a release. For so long in her life she had wondered about who her real parents had been. She had often wondered what it said about her that they had given her up.

For possibly the first time in her life she felt that she had experienced love before. It was overwhelmingly bittersweet. She felt the stirrings of anger in the depths of her soul. It helped to ground her as the rage churned that the parents she had never gotten to know had been stolen from her. She marched to the next closest door and slammed her hand against it.

It silently swung open to reveal that same landscape, but now everything was tinged with that unnatural red. She saw herself, probably around five years old, surrounded by other children her age. The scene reminded her of recess during elementary school as all the children crowded in a tight circle around a curiosity in the middle of the field. Alex sent her mind into that of her younger self who was on the inside edge of the circle.

She was so curious. *It looks kind of like us, but it is so weak*, she heard her younger mind try to puzzle out. The children had seen it climb through a hole in the ground beside the forbidden barn, and they ran over to investigate. Mr. Kragenn, the giant that taught them lessons, pushed his way through the children until he towered over the terrified creature. Mr. Kragenn began to teach them. *This*, his giant voice thundered, *is called a human. See how it resembles you?* Several students answered, *yeah,* and, *uh-huh,* in varying degrees of confusion. *It uses camouflage that makes it look like us as a defense mechanism. Does anyone remember what defense mechanism means?* He asked of them. Older Alex felt the smugness in her younger self's mind as her hand was the first one to shoot into the air.

Jessie, yes, what's the answer? He asked Alex. Older Alex was confused that he did not call her correct name so she dug through her younger self's memories until she understood. The brainwashing had started immediately after they had found her asleep in that cliff. Apparently they thought calling her by a different name would keep her away from the memories that may have developed at such a young age. She heard her younger self answering the question as she chased a barely discernable understanding in her young mind.

She followed it back to the same day her mother had been stolen away from her. Alex and her mother had been the only people in Ganeska that day who had not been connected to the ground at the moment that the earth beneath it had been tainted. When the Nephilim arrived in Ganeska they had sent a virus through the earth and the water that would immediately taint everyone within.

Alex was the only soul not affected who was still alive. Alex dug deeper for snatches of overheard conversations between the guardians when they thought she wasn't listening. Alex was amazed to find that there was far more than she would have thought, until she realized that it was a skill that young Alex had that she couldn't remember until now in her adult mind. Young Alex could hear the thoughts of everyone around her if they forgot to shield themselves, and could also hear conversations from many miles away.

The Nephilim thought it was so amusing every time Alex did something against her normal good nature. All the other children thought she was weird when she did something good. She saw a memory of a time when a huttingfly, a hummingbird and butterfly mix, had gotten stuck in the classroom one day. She had gone to it and cupped it in her hands and started toward the door with it. Mr. Kragenn had stopped her and angrily asked what she was doing.

She had calmly answered that she was taking it outside so it could go free, and he had started stomping toward her. She had cowered against the back wall. When he reached her, he had clapped his hands hard over her own. As the sticky blue, rose scented blood of the huttingfly had seeped between her fingers, he told her that they were evil creatures that sucked the blood from immortal children until they died.

Alex had known differently because she remembered seeing them drinking from the flowers, when the flowers still had colors, but she kept the knowledge to herself and went back to her seat as she kept her tears hidden in a deep closet in her mind. Ryder, the one kid who didn't seem to think she was weird and was still nice to her, leaned over and patted her hand with a sad face. Mr. Kragenn had kept her after class to discipline her after the incident.

Alex returned to her younger self's present and watched as Mr. Kragenn praised her for being correct. He then asked for her to step forward. He gently helped her step close to the specimen. *Now remove the defense mechanism, like we did with the frog in our last science class.* Young Alex stood staring down at this thing that looked a lot like them but with water running down its cheeks and a horribly scared face. She didn't want to do this, and she turned to Mr. Kragenn.

His eyes had become pinched, just like they always did before she did something wrong and he had to discipline her. She shied away from the memory of the beatings that she received when she did something wrong, but adult Alex felt the pain of every stinging lash from a cat o' nine tail that her young body had endured during those sessions. She went cold with rage and it seethed through her every pore, lighting her up from the inside out.

Young Alex turned to the specimen and drew her finger down through the air in front of it. As her finger cut through the air, so too did the skin peel away from the specimen. The noises became very loud and began to hurt her ears, while inside they seemed to scratch against her heart.

Then the noises stopped as the specimen fell onto its back on the ground. Mr. Kragenn sat beside the specimen and began to do an autopsy like they had on the frog as all the children greedily pushed forward for a better look. All but Alex. She pushed to the back of the crowd and willed herself to disappear, a new trick that she had learned just a few days before. She took off running to the clearing that she was always drawn to and curled up in the shrubs where she knew, no matter what anybody told her, there had been beautiful flowers before.

Her whole body felt like it was being squeezed of its own life, and she allowed her tears to pour out of her. She stayed there for only a short time because the teachers always came to look for her here if they couldn't find her. As she began to stand, she had a memory of a woman staring into her eyes. *Mother,* older Alex cried, but younger Alex had no recollection of her. She spoke, and the persuasion spread through her whole body until it screamed to be released.

You must escape this place once you are able. You will not be anyone's pawn, you are strong, the beautiful woman in her memory said to her. Young Alex stood and began to walk toward the waterfalls. She kept her invisibility going because she began to hear teachers calling for her. She reached the falls and peeked over the edge. It was a long way down; she couldn't even see the bottom.

Somehow she knew this was the way out. She heard giant footfalls begin to thread through the trees, and the fear in her was more than she could ever remember experiencing. She then realized these were Mr. Kragen's giant steps. Her decision was made, though. She jumped out into the void, and, as she went down, the persuasion finally left her with the final words from the woman, *You will forget this place and everything in it until you are ready.* Alex returned to her own mind.

Her tears had dried up and she had never been so angry. It felt like a ball of fire was burning through her soul. Still no exit appeared in the room, so she slammed her hand against the next door. That door opened up to the first foster home where she had been placed. It was right after they had taken her into their home for the first time. The woman was kneeling in front of her and going over the rules of the house. She was nice enough, but young Alex could tell that the woman, Allison, was holding something back. She sent her awareness out into the woman's mind. Alex saw that the woman desperately wanted a child to love. Allison had fostered three little girls so far that she had grown to love each time. Allison was worried about Alexandria leaving like they had done. All three of the girls had run away. Allison had tried so hard to help them and then to find them, but she had never found any trace once they left.

Alex liked the woman; she seemed like a genuinely kind person. Alex turned her attention to Allison's husband, Richard. He smiled very widely back at her. Alex sent her awareness into his mind and had to concentrate on not recoiling in horror. She saw each of the girls and the horrors Richard had put them through. Allison had no idea who she was married to.

With each of the girls they had fostered so far, he would be the perfect father for seven or eight months. Then his compulsions would kick in. He would put a sleeping aid in Allison's evening chamomile tea while she wasn't looking. Then he would go to their foster child's room. He would torture the girl for hours before killing her, letting her scream all she wanted because it made it more satisfying when she realized that Allison wasn't coming. He would then stage her exit. He was excellent at changing his handwriting so he would always leave a note for Allison to find the next day while he was "on a fishing trip." Then he would get rid of the body.

Alex saw all of this in just a second of looking through his thoughts. She became angry. She sent her mind back into his and began to distort every memory that he seemed to hold so dear. Instead of him being in control, she made him remember instead that he was being tortured in exactly the same manner by a shadow man.

She made him feel every moment of the torture he had put those girls through. She made him feel the terror of knowing how helpless he was. She pulled back from his thoughts and watched as those memories settled deep into his psyche.

He screamed incoherently at the top of his lungs, scaring Allison and causing her to go over to Richard to try to calm him. Over and over she asked him what was going on while he began to move around the house, banging through drawers and cupboards and closets, ripping things out of his way. Allison followed him to the bedroom, and Alex went to peek around the doorway.

His garbled words started to make sense. Over and over he was saying, "You let it happen" while he sobbed uncontrollably. Finally he found what he had apparently been searching for in the nightstand drawer. He didn't even hesitate. He pointed the gun at Allison and pulled the trigger and then put it against his own temple and pulled the trigger again. It was unnaturally quiet after the loud blasts from the barrel, and Alex stood in shock.

She ran to Allison and saw that the bullet had gone straight through her chest. Alex began to cry as she understood that she was the one at fault; she had caused this. It was too much for her five year-old mind, all of it had been. She should have never been able to see those things. She thought about hiding her abilities from herself but then remembered that she wouldn't have been able to see through Richard if she hadn't possessed them.

She concentrated very hard and somehow created an ability. She made her natural instincts become an ability to read a person's true character. Once that was done, Alex looked at the damage that she had created around her. She gathered everything in her mind about her abilities except for her instincts and threw them in a deep, dark room in her mind.

Alex was herself again. She turned to the rest of the doors. She searched for one that looked like it was in the worst shape. There had to be at least one hole in it because her ability to find anything that she was seeking had broken through, and she couldn't imagine that the door her six year-old self had created would be very sturdy.

There, that had to be it. One of the top corners of it had bowed out like something had pushed through. It was a thin wooden door, and it was barely clinging to the latch. When Alex placed her hand against it, the door didn't swing open like the rest. It latched onto her skin like it was part of her and quickly dispersed through her whole body. Alex fell flat on her back and everything went black.

Chapter Five: Hunting a Spy

Tristan had sat vigil beside Alex for hours. No matter what he tried, water, screaming, shaking, nothing would wake her. She hadn't moved or even twitched, but for a long while tears had steadily dripped from the corners of her eyes. That had stopped in the last hour or so. He heard the sound of several wings beating a landing outside on the balcony and remembered the meeting with his personal Guard. The one that he had set up before the whole world had been tipped upside down with the discovery of a Misakin on earth. He walked out to meet them before they could enter and stood protectively in front of the doors. "What have you found?" he asked. They all looked at each other in confusion.

"Don't you think we should discuss this somewhere more private?" Brandon asked.

Tristan knew he was right. "Yes, but there has been a serious change," he warned. They again looked to each other and shrugged their confusion. "There is... she...," he trailed off while he searched for the right words. His Guards had never seen him at a loss for words and were beginning to show signs of concern. "I found a Misakin." All of his men grabbed for their weapons while he tried to calm them.

"A Misakin on Earth? Shit, man, we haven't found the cure yet!

This could be the end of everything we've been working for!" Jackson exclaimed. All of the men began to talk over each other as they tried to think of ways to contain it.

"She's not infected!" He shouted to be heard. That shut them up for a second, but then Grant chimed in, "They were all infected. We had protectors waiting for refugees for two years. No one made it out of Ganesta."

"Somehow she did, and she's not infected." He held his hands up to stop the protests each of them looked like they were about to raise. "I know her. Brandon, do you remember that bar I took you to about 100 miles south of here? The Dive?" Brandon nodded. They had been discussing the battle from the night before at the time. "The bartender."

Brandon's eyes widened, "The hot one?" he asked incredulously.

"Not the redhead you were stuck on. The quieter one, smiled a lot. She hunted me down after the announcement. She is definitely a Misakin, but she has no idea what she is. I can't fathom how this occurred, but it did. I know she's not infected, though. She killed a Nefret demon and then when a Neshriki demon tried to take me out, she killed it.

It may have been too much for her to handle, though. She has been unresponsive for the last nine hours." His brow pinched in concern.

The men were quiet. "I feel a very strong urge to protect her that I cannot control. You may enter but do not attempt to approach her." Again they all looked at each other in confusion, but each nodded his head in agreement and put all weapons away.

Tristan led them through the doors and into the war room. There was a large oval table that took up most of the space in the room. The legs of the table and chairs appeared to connect directly to the floor. Jackson closed the doors behind him, and they all took chairs around the room. Brandon lifted his with a gentle tug and turned it the opposite way so that he could straddle the back. The roots spread to the floor beneath it again.

"Any news on our spy?" Tristan got right to the point of the meeting.

"I caught a trailing thread in the meeting with the officers this morning, but it dispersed when I tried to follow it. There's got to be more than one because it was meant as a communication. I'm sorry, boss," Jackson said.

Brandon leaned forward eagerly, "I caught it, too." All of them paid more attention at that, because Brandon was the best of Tristan's Guards at telepathy. "I didn't find the source," he warned, "but I was able to hear when it was received by one of the conspirators. I know who received it." Danger glinted in Brandon's eyes.

"The message was: 'The target has been spotted but lost. In transit toward New Hearth City. Eyes open for L.A.' Grantham was on the receiving end of that message. I held back on making my move until we could discuss it now. We still don't know who the other players are, and we don't have a clear number of the betrayers. We need a plan that will get Grantham to give away the others."

...

She awoke in a dark room, alone, but she could hear raised voices coming from a room close by. None was approaching, so she stared up into the dark. Her body was weak as though she had run for days. She sent her awareness out and knew that there were seven men in the next room. She listened in to the conversation as they discussed ways of getting information out of someone; torture, manipulation, etc.

She was concerned for a moment until she probed deeper and heard a name in Tristan's thoughts, Grantham. She swept the covers away and stood by the bed and stretched her tight muscles as she continued to listen. She caught the gist of what was going on. They seemed to be hunting a spy and had caught onto one of them but needed to find the others.

She reached into all of their minds at once and sent *Silly boys, there are easier ways to get the answers that you're looking for.* She

78

would swear that they all stopped breathing as they tried to throw up shields around their minds, but it was too late. She had crept into their minds and was too deep for the shields to block her.

She heard low growls coming from the room as she felt the men begin to reach for their weapons. They all stopped and made a conscious effort to remain still. She heard their confusion in their minds; apparently Tristan had never acted the way he was now. She decided to be kind and released herself from their minds as she reached for the doorknob and stepped into the hallway.

She walked confidently around the corner into the room with Tristan and what she had figured out was his personal Guard. She calmly walked to the remaining chair and sat with one leg crossed over the other. She almost laughed at the expressions of surprise on their faces but kept herself in check.

"When you're looking for a spy, you give them what they want the most. Then you send your best weapon to annihilate them," she said with a big smile. "Lucky for y'all, you have what they want. I'm Alex," she said into the quiet.

She could feel the distrust pouring out of Tristan's Guard like ants crawling on her skin as she waited calmly for someone to speak. She had seen enough of their minds to understand that if she showed any weakness or her confidence faltered at all in front of them, they would forever treat her as weak. With peripheral vision she saw Tristan's lips twitch like he wanted to smile.

Finally one of the men answered her. "I'm Brandon. Forgive us for being suspicious, but you took us by surprise." He had sandy blonde hair and tan skin. He looked like a surfer to Alex and had those same changeling eyes. Right now his were a suspicious, muddy brown.

"I am sorry that I pried into your minds. It was very rude of me. I had just woken up in a strange bedroom and heard a lot of men arguing about torture, a room away from me," she explained.

They all had the grace to look chagrined and another one spoke up, "Fair enough. I'm Simeon. We apologize if we scared you, but how did you get that far into our heads without us knowing? And all of us at once?" he asked abruptly.

Alex saw Tristan look at him sharply but she answered, "I'm still working that out myself; I just thought it and it happened." Jackson had thick red hair that curled slightly over his ears and an aristocratic face. Strong lines along his jaw, nose, and cheekbones. Alex realized that every single one of the men in the room was handsome, and each in a different way.

Tristan turned to her and asked quietly, "Are you okay? You've been out for a long time." She felt that anger and sadness from her time in her head try to rise up, almost glowing through her skin, and she pushed it down for a little longer. Not away, no closets in her head involved, just giving herself a little more time before she processed the rest of the memories that had poured into her mind once she had touched the door holding her power. "We'll talk later," she answered quietly as she resumed control of her emotions.

"So, what did you mean? What do you think our plan should be? I'm Jackson, by the way," another man spoke up. His eyes were currently a kind brown surrounded by hazel. He was gorgeous with dark bronze skin and thick black hair cut tight to his scalp.

Alex let herself enjoy the curling feeling of acceptance as she got back to the business at hand. "Nice to meet you, Jackson. First you have to find out what they are looking for. There's your bait. Then when a move is made to get to the target, you can take control of the situation and handle it."

"I agree," Brandon piped in. "Does anyone have any ideas on what the target might be?" He looked around the room. All of the men seemed to be thinking hard but not looking like they had found an answer. Brandon must have noticed her small smile. "You have an idea," he said.

She nodded slightly to him and addressed all of them. "So the message was about a target, L.A. as they called it, correct?" Several heads nodded in answer. "I know what your target is. It's me." Tristan looked sharply at her as the rest of them appeared to try to equate her with the initials L.A.

"Lost Asset. I am the only Misakin on Earth. There is nothing else they could be talking about," she explained.

She saw that they understood and Tristan spoke, "I thought you weren't aware of what you are."

"I definitely wasn't," she answered. "I've learned a lot of information while I was out. How long was I out, by the way?" "Nine hours." He looked like he wanted to ask questions but was impatiently holding himself in check.

Jackson spoke up again, "So you're the bait. How do we go about this? How do we draw out the spies?"

"When will you be addressing the public again?" she asked Tristan. "Early in the morning. Our own spies have gotten word to us that our enemies have begun to move again. The Dark Fae are marching through the Unseelie tunnels towards the surface, and the demons are collecting as many souls as they can from the outlying areas to get their strength up. We haven't heard from our spies in the vamp camps for a couple of days, so we don't know what they are planning. Toby," he spoke to the other Guard that she had not met yet.

He seemed to be very quiet and faded into the background, but once her focus was on him his presence seemed to overwhelm the room as he came to attention. Waking a sleeping dragon had never sounded more apt than now in Alex's mind. He had chestnut-colored hair cut in a professionally short style. He had an arresting face with a scruffy beard.

"I need you to meet up with our spies in the vamp camp, find out what the vampires are planning and why they have been unable to reach us." Tristan continued.

"I'm on it. It was interesting to meet you, Alex." He had a deep voice, the kind that seems to resonate in your bones. Being the focus of his attention, even if just for a moment, was disconcerting. "You, as well." she answered. He went to the balcony and Alex watched as his wings uncurled like magic from the blades of his shoulders. They were the richest jade color that she had ever seen. With an up and down beat of his wings he lifted into the air and disappeared. Alex brought her attention back to the meeting. "We need them to see me. Nothing overt, just a glimpse or something."

"Yes," Brandon was getting into the idea. "The cities are populated now. We need you to be in a large group so you can disappear quickly once you've been spotted."

"That won't work," Alex said. "They have to think that they've gotten what they want, if you mean to catch them all. We need to have them all trying to get to me; I can't just disappear. I'm going to get them to hunt me."

The guys all agreed and began to discuss strategy and logistics, trying to map out the city for her and figure out where men should be placed along her route. Tristan had been quiet for some time before Alex realized that he had not chimed in.

She turned to look at him and, as the other men did the same, the room became very quiet. He was unnaturally still and tensed for a fight. His hands were in fists. His skin seemed to shimmer in ripples showing dark onyx scales beneath it. His eyes were squeezed tightly shut and his mouth was turned down in anger.

She felt the men around her pull back and their minds glow behind their shields with understanding, but she was still confused. She gently reached out and placed her hand on his forearm. Tristan's eyes flashed open and stared directly into hers. She tried to pull back when she saw that his eyes had changed shape. They dilated like a cat's eyes would with a black oval surrounded by the iciest blue she had ever seen.

As she began to move her hand away he reached over and grabbed it with his own. Faster than she could comprehend he had carried her to the balcony, lifted her into his arms, and took flight. She was getting angry; she could feel it prickling just under her skin. He began to change form while they were airborne. His spine seemed to pop out into sharp silver spikes, and she went from being in his arms to being in his talons as his shape grew and adjusted. After just a minute or two, she was looking at the sleek onyx scales of Tristan's throat, and her anger began to spill out in her veins.

She tore through his mental shields, leaving them shredded on the floor of his mind as she yelled directly into his thoughts, "Put me down, asshole!" She felt the shock become a ripple straight through him, but he hadn't slowed yet. She couldn't grasp a coherent thought in his mind but she did feel his overwhelming urge to remove her from danger.

She was getting nowhere this way as his mind didn't seem to be involved in this runaway flight. She couldn't describe what she did. All she knew was she pulled back from him enough to witness the nerves firing off in his brain. She began to mentally flick the nerves. With the first nerve he faltered in the air and banked slightly left. He let out a frustrated growl and she flicked another one. This one caused one of his knuckles on his claws to release its grasp on her. He swung his huge dragon face to look down at her, and she swore she saw his eyes narrow in annoyance. She smirked back at him and flicked all of the nerves for his claws at once.

He let out a howl that sounded like fear as his silver-tipped claws released her, and she dropped in a freefall toward the earth. She relished the wind whipping past her face with almost childlike joy while he swung his large yet graceful body and put on speed to get beneath her. He got the tip of one of his wings beneath her and let her slide down the length of the leathery appendage to land on his back. She laughed in delight as she ran her hands along the soft scales on his back.

He began to descend to the nearest tower and landed with an unnecessary jolt. Alex slid down his foreleg to land on the spongy mesh of the roof and turned to face him. He was so beautiful, regal and commanding. He barked a growl at her and she thought, *and so angry*. He beat his wings once in frustration and her hair blew back from her face.

"I don't know what your deal is, but I can tell you that if you ever manhandle me like that again I will seriously make you regret it," she called out to him as rain began to beat down on her. His answer was to stomp one of those large forelegs. It shook the building and almost made her lose her balance. "You're acting like a two year-old having a tantrum. What the hell is your deal?"

She sent her awareness into his mind again, cringing slightly at the damage she had done to his shields. His thoughts were still chaotic, but the feeling behind them was clear. He was feeling seriously protective, like she was made of glass or something and that pissed her off all over again.

You don't know me, anything that I've been through, what I am, or what I can do. But I can promise you that I can take care of myself.

86

I don't need you! I'm trying to work with you, but I can do this without you, probably better without this kind of macho 'me Tarzan, you Jane' bullshit.

Dangerous, she got in response. *He was calming slightly if he could form actual words*, she thought to herself. She sent, *Yeah, I got that, but I am not a child; I am a grown woman, and I can decide on what I can and can't handle. And it really pisses me off that you just let your entire personal Guard see that you think I'm weak! You were the last person that I thought I needed to prove myself to, but I guess saving your life doesn't get any points with you!* She could feel the anger glowing through her skin and also realized that she was getting soaked while she yelled at him.

He shook his giant head and appeared to try to pull his wits back together. *That's not what they think*, she got back, but he had pulled his emotions back and she couldn't tell what he meant. She watched as he began to shrink back into his man shape. She felt his mind sharpening back to normal as he came back to himself.

"What else could they think?! They accepted that I had a valid reason to be a part of this and let me help with the strategy planning, and then you go crazy and drag me away like I'm some fragile flower that can't hang with the big boys! I have my own reasons for wanting to get to the bottom of who's behind this, and you are seriously infringing on my ability to do that. So just get out of my way and let me do this, or say goodbye and I'll handle it without your help. Far less dangerous that way, am I right?" she ended sarcastically.

She watched as he made a conscious effort to be rational again. He released his hands from rigid fists and drew a deep breath as he rolled his shoulders to release the tension there. He then stood up straight. He was still holding back everything in a tight, distant space in his mind. She tried to read what he was feeling but couldn't even get a glimmer; he was locked too firmly away in himself. "I will speak to them and make sure that they know you are to be treated as a valuable member of this action. I also truly apologize for what just occurred. I feel a very strong urge to protect you from danger. It is because you are a Misakin. They used to be considered treasured creatures to all of us, before..." he trailed off at that like he didn't want to finish the thought, so she finished it for him, "Before they were infected."

He looked at her and she could feel his curiosity reaching through that distant barrier. She shivered as a gust of wind reminded her that she was still getting soaked in the rain. He noticed her shiver from the chill wind and apologized again. "We should return so we can continue with setting up our plans. I would still like to speak to you about what happened while you were unconscious, but this is not the time." He looked hesitant and awkward after that.

"What? Why are you being weird?" she asked.

"I need to fly you back to Central Tower as we are many miles away from it right now," he shrugged slightly and held his hand out to her, "and I feel like you may still be perturbed by my treatment of you. Again I apologize, but I am going to have to carry you there and I don't want you to feel uncomfortable." She almost laughed but held it back. There he was, the slightly formal but honest Tristan that she had met earlier that she thought was his normal personality.

"It's fine, I would prefer to get back to the planning quickly. I'm not the type that will disregard expediency out of spite." She put her hand in his and he picked her up more gently than the last time. She was held close against his chest, and she looked up to watch those beautiful wings spread out from his back.

She saw a muscle in his jaw twitch, then he launched them into the air and back to his balcony. She relished the wind blowing by, even though she was freezing in her soaked clothes. With every beat of his wings they would drop slightly and then lift. He would occasionally catch a current and just glide with it, like an eagle with his wings held out to direct himself through the air. They landed far sooner than she wanted, but she was glad to be back. They had a lot to plan in a very short amount of time.

He put her down and she walked through the doors to the sitting room. Tristan's Guards came to attention as she walked in, followed by Tristan. She knew he had allowed her to enter first to establish her strength in their eyes, and she appreciated it.

"I apologize for my behavior. Treat Alexandria as one of us. I trust her to handle herself as should you." The men nodded their agreement and walked toward their seats.

"I need to pause the meeting for a moment though," Alex said. She turned to Tristan and asked, "Where may I be able to find some dry clothes?"

"I went back for your pack this morning after I got you safely here. Your things are in the closet of the bedroom you were in earlier."

"That was kind of you, thank you." She went to that bedroom and changed quickly. She tried to listen for anything coming from the other room, but it was quiet and all of their shields were in place. Even Tristan had repaired his shields, and held them tightly in place. She could feel tendrils of thought passing between them, though. She hoped he was making it clear that he did not think she was weak. She grabbed a towel from the linen closet next to the bathroom and dried her hair as best as she could, then went back to where they were meeting. When she entered the room, the tension had dissipated and the men were again at ease around her.

"Alright, let's get back to it," she said as she took her seat again. They spent several hours going through where she would be, where men would be positioned, and going through a hand-drawn map of the city until she knew it like the back of her own hand. They planned for possible scenarios of anything that could go wrong.

"Alright, it's time to get some sleep. Gentlemen, we'll begin at precisely ten a.m." Tristan said. The men stood and made their way to the balcony. Alex followed and watched as they all spread their wings and took off into the night. She was fascinated by the myriad colors on each of them, and as they disappeared she asked Tristan, "Do any of the Draigkin have the same colors?"

"No," he answered, "each Draigkin's coloring is unique and is as individual as a fingerprint." Something teased her memory but she was too tired to follow the thought. "I shouldn't feel this tired; I was out for so long today."

"Yes, but you weren't exactly resting peacefully," he answered.

"True. I believe I will grab some rest while I can. Thank you for letting them know that I could handle this."

"Of course. I know you are capable of handling yourself, and you're very intelligent. You were an asset in helping figure this out. Again I apologize for my behavior earlier," he replied.

"It's alright. Good night, Tristan." She began to walk toward the room where her belongings were stored.

He stopped her, "I would still like to ask you about what happened while you were unconscious and how you know what happened to the Misakin."

Her jaw popped on a yawn and she said, "I'm still processing some of it. Let me sleep on it, and I'll tell you everything I remember in the morning."

"Alright. Sleep well, Alexandria. I'll see you in the morning."

"Call me Alex." She smiled at him as she went to her bedroom and shut the door. She climbed into the decadently comfortable bed and passed out almost immediately.

Chapter Six: Overtaken

She awoke with the dawn. She got up and went to the attached bathroom to shower and get ready for the day ahead. She dressed and left her room to find for Tristan. He wasn't in the public areas, so she went to the door of the other bedroom. He was sleeping on his stomach, with one leg straight and the other pulled halfway up. His face was turned away from the doorway.

He was in pajama pants, but his shirt was precariously dangling from the edge of the bed. She was about to turn away and go to the kitchen to look for some kind of breakfast when she heard him begin to speak. It was so soft that she couldn't hear his words. He sounded angry, though. He began to slightly growl in between words. She guessed he was having an argument in his sleep and she walked forward to wake him.

She placed her hand on his bare shoulder and gently called his name. She felt an electric current travel up her arm and race just beneath her skin. She felt him go still beneath her hand. Then, faster than she could gasp in a breath, he turned and yanked her forward. She lost her footing and landed hard against him, and he turned them both until he was lying on top of her. She pushed at his shoulders to give herself room to get out.

Tristan's eyes were still closed and he laid his head between her shoulder and neck. He placed his lips gently against her neck just above her racing pulse and she felt herself go weak. She tried to inject a little strength into her voice when she called his name again. It came out more shaky and questioning than she wanted, but as she opened her mouth to try again he lifted his head and took her mouth with his.

It was an excellent kiss, soft and strong at the same time. His lips were soft against her own, and she closed her eyes and gave into it. His tongue slipped into her mouth and curled around her own. His hand came up and he pressed his thumb to her pulse as he lifted her face further into the kiss. Their tongues began to duel more insistently and she wrapped her arms around him. She ran her hands up his back and pressed herself into him as those tingles raced through her system. He went tense under her fingers and broke the kiss.

Alex opened her eyes. He was staring down at her with confusion and some other emotion she couldn't figure out with soft violet-colored eyes. She felt herself blush under his gaze, and she pulled her hands around to his shoulders and gently pushed. He quickly sat up, still watching her but giving her room to get up.

She got out of the bed and looked down to straighten her shirt as she pulled her thoughts together. "I'm so sorry," he began, and she looked up, shocked.

"If anyone should apologize, it's me. I'm sorry, you sounded like you were having a bad dream. I shouldn't have entered your bedroom." She looked to the door and prepared to make her escape. "It was my mistake, not yours. I'll let you get ready for the day. I'll see you shortly." She hurried out of the room and escaped to the kitchen. She pressed her hands to her flaming cheeks and tried to figure out what just happened.

It doesn't mean anything. Pretend it didn't happen. That's the best approach; he didn't seem pleased about it anyway, it's for the best. She continued to recriminate herself for going into the room at all. *Forget it*, she told herself firmly. She looked in the refrigerator and grabbed some eggs. She looked on the counters and found some bread, then looked in the cabinets until she found a skillet. She heated up some 'eggs in a basket' and she pushed what had just happened out of her mind.

She prepared a plate for herself and for Tristan and took them to the sitting room. She had just placed the plates on the table there when she felt him enter the room behind her. She calmly sat in front of her plate and pulled it closer. He was still quiet as he stood in the doorway. She looked up at him and gestured to the plate she had made for him.

"It's nothing fancy, just fried eggs inside toast, but it's pretty good." He was staring at her, so she looked back to her plate and picked up her knife and fork. He walked over to the couch and sat beside her. He seemed to be waiting for her to look at him, so she turned her head toward him.

"I would like to…" he started to say, but she cut him off.

"There's no need for you to apologize, I told you, it was my fault. Let's just forget it happened," she said.

He growled softly under his breath. "Not what I was going to say. I would like to… oh for God's sake," he said, and then he pulled her into a drugging kiss. No sleepiness in this kiss; it was carnal and almost savage in its intensity. He grasped her long hair in a fist and pulled her head back to get deeper into the kiss. She melted, no other way to describe it, and her mind instinctively reached out to his. Their minds collided, and she could feel everything that he was feeling.

Elation, lust, and awe stood out in his mind. Elation and awe that he had found her. She tried to follow the thought because it had a deep meaning for him. She caught the word Kahlicor. *What does it mean?* She asked him. He didn't answer just pulled her even closer and began to explore in her mind. He found the memories that she had recently had to face and gentled against her lips.

She grew embarrassed and pulled away. She came back to herself and felt a tear slide down her cheek. She tried to discreetly wipe it away while she looked away from him. He gently pulled her face back to him. She cringed, waiting for the judgement that she expected to see for some of the things that she had done. It never came, and, instead, he just looked at her steadily with sympathy in his eyes. "I'm sorry," he said quietly. She thought maybe he meant sorry for the kiss, so she pasted on a fake smile and said, "No, it's fine, curiosity satisfied." She turned to her now cold food.

"No, never for that," he said adamantly, and she realized that they were still somehow connected in their minds. He pulled her to him and wrapped his arms around her. "For what you had to face alone. I'm sorry for what you went through. I wish I had been there, so that you had someone to help you deal with everything that you were subjected to at such a young age. I don't know how you've turned out as well as you did, but I'm so grateful that you did."

She hid her face in his chest and said, "Did you not see the other things? I didn't come out well. I sent a girl to an asylum for the rest of her life for being mean to me a couple of times. I've killed people." Tears slid slowly down her cheeks. He began to gently stroke her hair.

"You did come out well. We all have skeletons in our past. You never had anyone to understand; even you couldn't understand how different you were. I have seen your strength of character and your will. You know who you are and where you stand now. You're an amazing person because of what you've done in the past, not in spite of it."

She wiped her cheeks and lifted herself back up. "Thank you." She looked to the balcony doors and saw the sun was a little higher in the sky. "Almost that time," she said as she faced him again. "I guess we need to talk about this," she gestured between them, "but I think we should concentrate on the mission."

"I agree. My Guard should be here soon." He looked at the plate that she had made for him. "Thank you for breakfast. Would you like me to heat these up?"

"Nah, it's not really a dish that heats up well. I'll just grab something a little later." She heard the sound of wings and turned to see Tristan's Guards arrive on the balcony. Tristan stood and went to open the doors for them. They filed in, and Alex could feel the adrenaline sparking through them. It was contagious, and she felt her own excitement and adrenaline start to flow faster. After a few minutes of small talk even though everyone was anxious to go, Tristan finally gave the nod to proceed.

Alex left the apartment through the front door while Tristan and his guard left from the balcony. They all kept their camouflage in place in the air and took off for their positions. Alex took the elevator down to the lobby and walked to the front doors. She took a deep breath and released it as she pushed through the doors. There were a lot of people on the streets. More than she had thought there would be. She followed the path that they had decided on the night before and made her way to the city center where a marketplace had been set up once the city had become populated. She got there and began to wander leisurely through the stalls, mini-versions of the large towers, just not as many decorative minerals and metals on them.

She heard Brandon's voice in her mind, *There's Grantham. He's at the vegetable stall, two ahead from your position to the left.* She made sure not to turn her head and looked through her eyelashes toward that position.

Description, she requested back. There were two men in that area, one pale with sun bleached short hair and the other with tan skin and rich sienna-colored hair. She couldn't see either man's face.

The taller one with darker hair, he replied.

Got it, she sent back.

She began to walk to the next stall when she heard a questioning, "Alex?" She was confused about the feminine voice calling out to her in the middle of the operation and looked around quickly. She caught the flash of a very familiar smile as Sierra came running toward her.

"Oh, my God, I was so worried! Thank goodness you're here!" Sierra threw her arms around her and squeezed until Alex worried about her ribs. "I didn't know if you would make it! Where have you been? I was so scared!" Sierra started to cry against her shoulder, and Alex tried to calm her.

"Shh, Shh, It's all okay. I'm here, I'm alive," Sierra stepped back, keeping one arm locked around Alex's arm and wiped her cheeks. "Sorry, you know me," she laughed quietly. Sierra smiled and said, "You gotta tell me what you've been up to.

Come on, you gotta see this place I'm staying at. I swear, it's magical!"

"Most definitely," Alex laughed. "Can we meet a little later, though? I've got to finish something I'm working on; it's important. Two hours we'll meet right here. Okay?" Sierra's smile slipped a little, and Alex finally noticed the panicked look in Sierra's eyes.

"Just come see my place so you know where you can find me, is that okay?" She pleaded silently with her eyes.

"Sure," she answered after a beat. Alex saw relief in her friend's eyes and allowed her to pull her towards a tower nearby. She had lost sight of Grantham and sent a mental call out to Brandon, "In trouble, no contingency plan. My best friend is here and panicked. I've got to find out what's going on, I have a feeling it may have something to do with the mission, I need backup. Make sure someone stays right on us." They walked inside and Alex followed

Sierra to the elevator doors. "Can you talk yet?" she asked under her breath.

"So where did you go from my house? And from that little grocery store that you like so much?" Alex felt her skin go cold. Sierra couldn't have known that Alex would have stopped at George and Edith's. They walked onto the elevator and the doors slid quickly shut behind them. Alex sensed movement near Sierra but couldn't figure out why. There was no one except the two of them on the elevator.

As the lift began to ascend Sierra slumped bonelessly to the floor. "Sierra!" Alex screamed. She fell to the floor to lift Sierra's upper body onto her lap. She brushed her hair to the side and checked her pulse. Where is it? Where is it? Alex was quickly panicking as she tried to find Sierra's pulse. She laid her back on the floor of the lift as she realized with horror that the reason she couldn't find her pulse was because there wasn't one.

She began to apply pressure on Sierra's chest over and over. She leaned over to check and see if Sierra was breathing but couldn't feel any breath against her hand. She tilted Sierra's head back to open her airway and tried to breathe life back into her lungs. Still no breath, so she switched back to compressions as tears began to burn in her eyes. *No, no, no, no, no*, just kept repeating in her mind. The elevator doors opened onto a suite, and two men came into the elevator and pushed Alex back. One of them lifted Sierra in his arms, walked off the elevator, and entered a room of the suite. The other followed and slammed the door behind them.

"What are they doing with her? She needs a hospital, now!" Alex demanded of the shadow that had appeared in the hallway in front of her. She was edging very quickly into hysteria. Tears raced down her cheeks.

"Impressive, you can see me now. It did take you a minute though." The shadow shimmered into a more corporeal darkness, like a silhouette. Alex's tears burned down her cheeks, "Answer the question!"

"She served her purpose. She has moved on to a better existence now. I needed to speak with you, and she was kind enough to indulge me," it answered. It cocked its "head" to the side as it watched her. Alex felt rage rising inside of her as she began to understand that this being had taken away her only true friend in this world. She focused all of her building rage toward the condescending entity before her. Her body lit up, and she felt like fire was racing through her veins. She looked down for a moment and realized her skin was aflame on her arms and hands. She pictured the door in her mind that had held all of her gifts and potential and grasped the handle tightly.

She pulled the door open and let it wash through her. She focused her rage and sent it flying toward the shadow. It looked like a sonic blast moving through the air just before it slammed into him. Alex didn't know what to expect from it, but she certainly didn't expect what happened. When that blast of rage struck it, the Shadow laughed. It laughed! Then it appeared to grow larger than it had been before. Its pleasure curled through the air as it turned back to her.

"Oh, this is going to be so much fun!" it exclaimed happily. "The possibilities are endless! Now, come along, my dear, we don't have much time." He turned to the hallway behind him. "Ryder, you're up." The name struck her first. The shadow before her disappeared and Alex looked toward the footsteps approaching from the left, out of eyesight from inside the elevator.

Alex pulled herself up using the wall of the elevator and readied another blast. Whoever walked around the side of that elevator would have flesh and bones; perhaps that's why it didn't work on the shadow man. The footsteps slowed, and a man stepped into her line of sight. She released that ball of rage with a primal yell. Just as it made contact with the man the shadow had named Ryder, she recognized him with heart-stopping surprise.

Toby, one of Tristan's guards, smiled widely at her as he absorbed the rage. Alex could see the dragon under his skin, and she saw its movements as it sat up in curiosity. Ryder chuckled softly and stepped into the elevator. Alex backed as far into the corner as she could as he came at her.

He crowded into her personal space and placed his hands to either side, effectively caging her in. His eyes roamed over her face then he leaned even closer, until they were almost touching noses. His pupils were edging into that oval shape of his dragon form and the iris was a deep maroon color.

"Hello, Jessie." He whispered. The name from her time in Ganeska shocked her. It also reignited her anger and grief, and she spit in his face in an effort to get him to back away.

"I've missed your fire, Jessie, but now is not the time for flirting," he said as he wiped her saliva from his face. Then, without warning, he picked her up in a fireman's hold. Before she could take a breath to verbally tear into him, he strode off of the elevator and down the hallway.

Alex was kicking, screaming, and punching against his back as he turned and entered what appeared to be a study. He threw her unceremoniously onto a couch in the room and walked behind the desk. As she scrambled to get to her feet, he appeared before her in a blink and pushed her back down on her back.

He quickly bound her feet, knees, and wrists with rope. He grinned down at her as she stewed in her own venom. He stooped down and pressed his lips to hers in a blindingly quick peck. Sparks flew through her mind and body like fireworks and then he pulled back.

It was enough to stun her into silence, and he had the audacity to wink at her as he stood upright.

The shadow man appeared behind the desk. "Thank you, Ryder, that will be all for now." Ryder, or "Toby", whatever his name was, nodded toward the manifestation and exited the room.
"Now that that's out of the way, we need to have our little chat." Alex wiggled into a sitting position as she tried to think.

"What are you?" she asked.

"I'm a Shade. You can call me Varone," he said. He came around the desk and perched on the corner. "And you are a Misakin, here on earth. How marvelous!"

"You killed my best friend, and I'm going to rip you to shreds, how marvelous," She replied, deadpan.

"Oh, that, I already told you, she went to a better place." He dismissed that with a wave of his insubstantial arm. Alex opened her mouth to speak but he continued. "If you want to see her again... alive... then we need to talk." Alex kept quiet.

"Good. She is alive, not in this dimension, of course, but I can teach you how to find the pathway into Bakholm. Here's what I need in return. You're going to play a vital part in the next part of this war... on my side. You are going to make sure that I win or you will never see your friend again. Or, incidentally, your mother." Alex remained quiet as those stunning words settled into her mind. Her mother. He was saying that she could meet her mother.

"I will give you twenty-four hours to make your decision. If you decide that the temptation is just not enough, then I will let you return to your new friends. They can't win this war, by the way, with or without you. I've been preparing this design for centuries. Just say my name once you have decided on your course of action." He then disappeared, no flash or fancy, just gone. She had so many thoughts, and they just kept circling through her mind at dizzying speed. Names, dimensions, monsters, the reshaping. Faster and faster they flashed through. Betrayal, attraction, anger, determination, sadness.

Then the door opened and that bastard walked in, Ryder. Her thoughts sharpened into the sharpened tip of a spear. As he turned to close the door behind him, she let it fly. She watched as a spear manifested in her line of sight, flying straight toward his heart. Just before it would have slammed into him, he seemed to appear across the room and the spear slammed into the doorframe instead.

He moved so quickly that it looked like a blur, and he was suddenly directly in front of her. He was kneeling to keep her eyes level with his own, and his shone with the excited yellows and oranges of the sun. "This should be very fun." He said with a wide smile.

Chapter Seven: Alternate Endings

"What happened? How could you lose her?!" Tristan yelled at his second in command. His Guards were all subdued with disappointment about the failure of their mission. Tristan was feeling a lot of things, but disappointment wasn't among them. Overwhelming fury was the main one, followed by desperation and absolute terror. None of them had any idea where Alex was or what the Shadow faction had planned for her.

"She was doing well, she had Grantham in view. She was about to approach him and she disappeared. I couldn't connect to her mind anymore, and she was just gone. I went to where she had been and even her scent was gone. There was no way to track her. We searched nearby buildings and all over the market." He ran his hands through his hair in agitation. "Even Grantham was gone, same thing, and we can't find him, either. I'm so sorry boss."

Tristan turned and walked away from them as he tried to rein himself in. His skin was rippling as his inner dragon tried to force its way out to go find her. He talked himself down because they had nowhere to go and no leads to hunt down. He also couldn't destroy his friends with the fury that his dragon would spew at them for just being near him right now. He could feel their fear of him losing control and destroying them. Which, oddly, served to help him put the feelings away. He composed himself and walked back to the sitting room where his Guard was waiting.

"What do your sources say?"

"No one knows where they're keeping her, but the rumor that a Misakin has been found on earth is circulating all across their front lines. It seems to have stopped the advance for now. Good and bad news, I guess. We have the time to find the humans that are hiding and get them to the safety of the hearth cities, but what good does it do for our enemies if they stop right now?" Grant questioned.

Tristan thought for a minute. "Exactly. We have too many questions and not enough answers. Talk to your sources. Find the answers that we need. I don't trust this pause, and we need to know what they are waiting for. Push them to dig deeper. We need to know what they have planned for Alexandria. Go. I expect you to return immediately if you find out anything." He met each of his guard's eyes. "I cannot stress to you how important she is to the future of this world. Find her, or we fail."

They bowed deeply and left in a hurry to get to their sources. Once the sound of their wings had disappeared, Tristan finally allowed his anger to surface again and he roared to the sky. After several minutes he stopped. He fell to his knees and let the terror run amok in his mind as he imagined horrible scenarios that could be Alex's current situation.

"No. None of it. She is alive and she is fine. She hasn't been harmed," he heard a feminine voice say softly. Tristan turned, pulling his blades from their sheaths in an instant, but he saw nothing. He walked back to the sitting room and stood poised to spring. He saw a hint of movement in the far corner and watched as a shadow grew subtly more substantial until it became the silhouette of a woman.

"I mean you no harm, quite the opposite in fact." She held her shadowy hands up in supplication.

"Who are you?" he demanded.

"Selaina. I'm on your side." She dropped her arms back to her sides. He couldn't smell her. He couldn't get any kind of read on her, and it was disconcerting.

"What are you? Why can I not read you at all?"

"I am a Shade. You can't read me because I'm not technically here. My kind can't leave our own dimension, but we can project our spirits elsewhere. You need my help."

"How do you know anything about Alexandria?"

She laughed softly. "Because my competition has a big mouth."

"Competition?" he was getting more confused.

"Where I'm from, war is art. We feed off of the chaos of death and destruction, and war provides the most sustenance for us.

Ages ago, our leaders decided to make it a competition for the greatest piece. Two Shades, two sides at war. The competitors choose a side, and whatever side comes out the winner earns the Crown for a period of time. The winning side is considered the artistic piece, and our bards sing of their fight until the next meal is needed and the next competition begins. It was smart. We were losing too many of our own people in attempted coups." She stopped and waited for him to process that.

"So you live off of death. Innocent or evil, doesn't matter," he said with disdain.

"Hey! I can't help my biological makeup, so stop the judgement and suck it up. If it makes you feel better, I don't like the taste of an innocent's death. Too bitter for me, though I can't say the same for my competitor. Now ask me the right question."

He thought for a moment. "Your competitor has a big mouth, and that gives you an insight into his strategy. That calls to mind many questions, but the first is, where is Alex?"

"Nope, wrong question. I can't give out locations, it's against the rules."

"What is he planning to do to her, then?" he put his blades away as he asked.

"He won't harm her for now. She's a weapon of mass destruction if he can convince her to fight for his side."

"And if he can't?" he asked. He was remembering all of the good that radiated from her character.

"He will kill her, and I don't mean that she would move on to Bakholm. He will destroy her soul so that she could never find her way back. She has already escaped one dimension. He would not give her the chance to do so again."

Tristan's heart constricted at the thought of her death. "It's not in her to let herself fight for him." His airways closed up and he walked to the sofa and sat down hard as grief rose up in a tidal wave. Just before it would have crashed over him, she answered.

"She might, and therein lies the good and the bad news. He has something that she wants, something that she needs more desperately than even she knows. Good news is he gave her time to decide. Bad news is that if she fights for his side... then yours will lose."

Hope pushed back the grief. "How much time do we have before she has to decide?"

"Right around twenty-two hours left, but she can call his name anytime in the interim if she comes to a decision."

"Can you give me any information that would point me in the right direction?"

"You Draigkin rely too much on your abilities sometimes. Go back to the market. Ask the people that you are trying to protect. There is information there that was missed. My competitor, Varone, should be checking in at court soon. There will be information spread to my spies, and I will return to you when I learn anything that I am allowed to pass on. I may also have one trick up my sleeve" She disappeared.

We have intel, I'm on my way to check it out. Continue with your efforts and meet me back at the tower in one hour. We have only a small window of time to get to her, he sent to his Guards. He went to the balcony and took off for the market as he heard the chorus of agreements from his men.

"Go to hell," Alex responded.

"Been there, done that, love," he answered. "I'm going to cut your bonds now. Please tell me you're going to be a bad girl and keep trying to kill me. I love the foreplay."

Alex's nose wrinkled in disgust, "You're sick, or brain damaged. How did you survive the blast I hit you with? And you're supposed to be one of the good guys, Toby! How did you get pulled to the dark side?"

He barked out a laugh, "I wasn't tempted to the dark side. I am the dark side. How do you think they knew about you? I saw you, outside of a house south of here." Alex remembered the beautifully terrifying colors of the dragon that roasted Sierra's home with a pang of grief. Ryder pulled out a knife and began to cut through the bonds on her legs. "And your little tantrum can't harm me in here. Any violence directed toward us in this warded penthouse only makes us stronger."

"So, what, Toby? You knew what I was by looking at me? Thought I might make a good weapon for you and your cronies?" Alex asked with anger in her voice. He looked up from cutting her bonds and met her eyes with emerald colored irises quickly flickering to dragon and back.

"Don't call me Toby again," he said with temper in his voice to match hers.

"Why, Toby? It's the name you told the people that you are betraying. Feeling ashamed?" she asked with disdain.

He slammed the knife into the sofa beside her as he leaned forward and crowded her into the back of the couch. "My name is Ryder, and, no, I don't feel ashamed at the naiveté of those ridiculous creatures." The name struck her again as familiar. "Yes, you do know me," he answered her unspoken question.

She didn't recognize him and knew her confusion was showing. He growled his frustration, then put his hands to either side of her face before she could get her bound hands up to protect herself. An electric pulse traveled from his hands through her body to her toes and back. He slammed his lips to hers as he mentally pushed a memory into her mind.

He was trying to keep up with his dad, his little legs taking three steps for each long stride of his father's. He saw a little girl in one of the gardens and came to a stop. She seemed to be trying to take her first steps and she looked so happy. He was already able to run, so in his mind he needed to help her because it was his duty as a big boy.

He toddled over to the little girl. She looked at him and smiled really big and held her hand out as she started to fall. He grabbed her hand. Time stopped. He felt his heart beat hard, and something in him reached out to her. Her mind grabbed onto it, just as she had grabbed his hand, and held it tight. He knew he could never be whole again without her. She grinned back at him as she fell into his arms and patted his face when he caught her.

Ryder kissed her as a punishment. Violence, lust, and desperation meeting in a kaleidoscope of sensation. She bit his lip hard enough to draw blood and used all of her strength to push him away. He sailed across the room and hit the far wall with a crack of bone. She stood, breathing hard, and wrangled the bonds from her wrists as he stood and began to laugh. She wiped her mouth with the back of a wrist and spit his taste out of her mouth. He mirrored her movements, spitting blood from his bleeding lip, and smiled widely at her.

"Your mother must be so proud of your caveman attitude. You touch me again without my permission and you will die. I don't care who you are," she said forcefully.

"Good. You're learning quickly that you can't care about who you're fighting while at war. That was lesson one." Alex saw red. "Training? You're trying to teach me how to go to war?" she seethed.

"We both know that you're going to fight. Whichever side you end up taking, you will be an integral piece in the game."

"Why are you doing this? Protecting humans is in your genetic makeup. Why work with these people who want to destroy them?"

"It's not destruction, it is order. The other side has already rounded up the humans for us and put them in their paddocks. They will be treated well, like prized cattle. These people don't want to kill them all like you think. Most of this faction can't survive without them. Believe it or not, I am protecting them. Humans kill each other off all the time, for the most ridiculous of reasons. By controlling them, we can put an end to their needless suffering. They will still live on. They'll still have warm beds, food, and the ability to procreate," he answered. The warm honey brown of his eyes showed her he sincerely believed what he was saying.

"Wow, you certainly did drink the Kool-Aid, didn't you? Treated like prized cattle? In your dreams, more like blood slaves and brood mares. These people won't allow humans to just go on about their lives; it doesn't make any kind of strategic sense. They outnumber the monsters by billions! Use your brain!" she ended on a yell.

"Yes, well, of course the bad meat needs to be destroyed before it can poison the rest of them. There will be a purge and then the world will become much simpler. Hell, it will be paradise," he answered calmly.

"Until they become dinner for a ravenous vampire or something."

"Yes, well, such is life. Everything needs sustenance. Don't you enjoy a good steak every once in a while? Do you worry about the mental health of that cow as they slaughtered it? Or the feelings of other cows in the herd for its absence afterwards?"

"I cannot agree with your vision of the future," Alex said.

"Then leave," he answered calmly. "But know when you do that you will never be reunited with your friend or mother." Alex's heart constricted at the mention of them, and the fight left her for a moment as she bowed her head.

"Or you can get off your high horse and accept that this world is already an ugly place. Why not make it easier to function in it? The plan that those do-gooders are trying to establish, running individual towns like the renewal of the feudal system with a mix of democracy, can never work. The same problems are going to remain. Jealousy, greed, ambition, racism, bigotry, murder. These feelings are the human condition. Without the fear, the world will never be safe," he said.

It almost made sense, if you were psychotic. She sat down on the sofa and looked at him. She needed to think, but she needed to know, "How did you make it out of Ganeska, Ryder?"

He was quiet for a moment as he watched her. "I saw you go over the waterfall and I followed you." His eyes were a guarded chocolate brown, and she knew this would be his only response.

"What you showed me… is that supposed to mean something?" she asked, but he remained quiet.

"Fine. I need to think. Can you go away now?"

"No," was all he answered. She felt her temper trying to rise again.

Why was it so easy for him to get a rise out of her? She tamped it down and turned away from him. She stood and walked to the bookshelves along the walls behind her. She ran her fingers along the spines of the books. She felt the prick of static electricity when they came into contact with a large red tome, so she pulled it from the shelf. There was no title or markings anywhere on the outside, so she opened it to the first page.

"What are you doing?" he asked.

"I thought that was pretty obvious, I'm ignoring you," she answered distractedly as she tried to make sense of the words on the page in front of her. It was another language, one that she had never seen before, but the words were blurring, changing before her eyes into recognizable script.

"How very adult of you," he answered with frustration. *A History of Angels and their Offspring* became clear to her as the words finished taking shape. This she could use.

"Fine, I will give you some time to think. I'll go grab some food for us, perhaps a big juicy steak," he said snidely. He strode to the door of the study and exited, slamming the door behind him.

Open your mind, Alexandria, she read. She felt the persuasion behind the words, and her mind expanded without her conscious thought. The door in her mind swung wide open, and power and knowledge collided. Alex laughed out loud in delight as she finally understood her mission. She placed the book back in the space it had occupied and stretched as her power became a Focus inside of her. She watched as the Focus curled around her right arm and became a picture of a dragon, but not like any that she had seen before.

One feathered wing curled over her shoulder, the other curving around her bicep. The wings shimmered with the same coloring as the rest of the powerful figure, but looked more like the form of her mother's beautiful angel wings than what she expected after seeing dragon wings. The body of it was sleek but powerful. The talons at the end of its four muscular legs and claws grasped tightly to her skin. Soft scales covered her dragon's form with sharp spikes curling all along her spine. The face of the creature was beautiful in its terrifying intensity. A long snout and angular features with spikes traveling down its forehead to just meet the top of its snout. It was pure silver in color, with thin, almost invisible curls of every shade of blue in strange symbols all over. The bright violet iris surrounding an oval-slitted pupil in its one visible eye made its femininity obvious.

She ran her fingertip along one of the feathered wings and could feel the silky softness of it. She heard his approach before the door opened to the study. He was clutching his right bicep as he came in, and his eyes collided with the Focus that had appeared on hers. His eyes opened wide in shock and snapped up to her own. His were flashing between the jade of his dragon's eyes and a shocked, and stormy, gray.

"Reading is so good for you. Knowledge is power, as they say," she quipped. She walked toward him as he backed up to the door that had closed behind him. She stopped just before him, and he looked at her with golden predator eyes. "Are you frightened of me now?" she asked softly.

"Perhaps there is a little of that, but that's not entirely what I'm feeling right now," he answered her just as softly with a raw undercurrent in his voice. She looked at him with a hint of pity.

"Do you miss the colors, Ryder?"

"What?" he asked with confusion.

"In Ganeska. I miss the colors, but I suppose you wouldn't. You were infected, so the blood of our parents that taints everything there now wouldn't have bothered you. I think you need to remember the colors." She placed her hand to his chest, just above his heart.

She pushed her power into him and followed its path with her mind. She directed it to every molecule that was shrouded in darkness and breathed new light into them. Tendrils of the evil that had infected him screamed inaudibly as they disintegrated in the new brightness until they were all gone.

She came back to herself and saw him slumped against the wall, unconscious. She heard footsteps approaching. She lifted him easily in her arms and walked to the double doors behind the desk. With a thought she opened them then sent her consciousness into her new focus. As she took on her new form she wrapped them both in camouflage and lifted into the air.

Chapter Eight: Preparing for Battle

She flew to the tower where she had met Tristan's Guard and landed on the balcony. She returned to her normal form before she dropped the camouflage surrounding her and Ryder. Once she was visible she heard a shout go up from the sitting room. The doors burst open and Tristan stepped onto the balcony, shock on his features. "Simeon, get Toby to a bed and find out if he's hurt." Simeon grabbed him out of her arms and walked back into the apartment.

"We were preparing to go rescue you. We finally found a witness in the market that saw you enter Oasis Tower. How did you get here?" he asked with appropriate confusion.

"I was aided by our hidden ally." She turned to the corner of the balcony and spoke to the Shade concealing itself there. "Thank you for your help. I am whole now, and I know what my mission is." The Shade appeared and bowed deeply to Alex. "You are welcome, Misakin."

"How did she aid you?" Tristan asked as he turned his gaze back from the Shade to Alex.

"She sent a compulsion to find a book that she had left for me. I lacked the knowledge to use my power until then." Tristan's eyes fell to the new Focus on her arm. It briefly turned its head to watch him with both eyes before settling back into its previous position.

"Your Focus is in your form? Every enemy soldier will know where to hit to kill you," he said with concern.

"Misakin, remember? It would take far more than destroying my Focus to kill me." Her Focus traveled lightning fast to her other arm and mirrored its previous position there, peeking around to stare him down before settling into its new perch.

"How is it doing that? Like it has a mind of its own?" he asked in astonishment.

"Because it does," she answered. "We must get to business, Tristan. Varone will have realized that I'm gone by now, and he'll notice that Ryder is missing as well."

"Who's Ryder?" he asked with confusion.

"Call your Guard to the war room and we will go through it all. I'll grab some food and meet y'all there. Shade," she said as she turned to look at her, "What is your name?"

"Selaina."

"Selaina, please join us." When she nodded her agreement Alex walked toward the kitchen. She needed protein and calories before she crashed. She found a plate of leftover chicken and mashed potatoes, so she heated them up with a thought and scarfed them down quickly. She immediately felt stronger. She washed and dried the dish and left it on a mat on the counter to dry, then headed to the war room.

She arrived just as Simeon was coming from a bedroom toward the meeting.

"So the mojo is working? About time, a woman your age should know who she is by now," he chuckled as they walked in and took their seats.

"Thanks," she answered drily, understanding that his teasing masked relief that she was unharmed.

"Alright, let's get to it," Tristan began. "What happened, Alex?"

"They knew our plan to go after Grantham to try to find the spy. They had a trap set for me when I started to make my move. My friend," her throat closed up for a moment and she coughed to clear it, "Sierra. He did something to her; she's alive, but he hid her in another dimension, Bakholm. But she's safer there than she would be here. I say we have less than an hour before the front lines arrive. Varone is aware that I'm gone. He may not know that I am at full power, so we have an advantage there. But he will not want to give you any time to prepare me for war."

"It makes sense. He was going to kill you if you didn't agree to join him, and you are a powerful weapon, so he worries about his ability to win if you join his enemy. He would rather win dirty than lose; he has more than just the normal competition at stake," Selaina said.

"What do you mean?" Tristan asked.

"Varone has begun a campaign to keep the Crown, once he wins it, back in our world. He's made a lot of promises to a lot of very powerful Shades. If he loses, he dies."

"I figured he had lied about letting me go. He also just lost his master spy, so he'll be angry at the loss of intelligence and strike blindly."

"Master spy?" Tristan questioned coldly as he looked toward the bedroom where Ryder had been placed. He moved like lightning toward the door of the war room, but Alex beat him there with her eyes flashing silver back at him.

"You will let it go," Alex demanded, staring him down.
"You're joking. He's been giving our secrets to our enemy and you want me to let him go? Not a chance in hell."

"You will let it and him go. He is not just one of your Guard. He is one of mine, and he is under my protection now. His father was stationed in Ganeska with the honor guard protecting the portal, and he was my friend. He was infected with the vile disease that was sent into my homeland. He is cured now. He needs to recover and you will leave him in peace. Do you understand?" she asked forcefully.

She could tell he didn't like it, but he accepted it. He walked back to his seat and sat down. He appeared to realize what she had said and his eyes lit up at a new thought. "You found a cure?" he asked excitedly.

"I am the cure, it's one of the things that I recently discovered," she replied. "We can get into later; we need our allies here now. We don't have much time," she said.

"Agreed. Go rally the forces, gentlemen." His guard left quickly and Tristan followed them out to the balcony.

"A word, please, Alexandria." Selaina stopped her as she began to leave. "You spoke of your homeland and the plague that spread through it. I can tell you who let the Nephilim in. It was Varone. Shades have the knowledge of how to open all of the portals, and in war we almost always play the long game. I believe he planned the attack on your homeland leaving only you uninfected on purpose, believing that he could convince you to fight by his side," she said sadly.

Alex could see it, the long game and the moves that would lead to this very moment and building up to war. "He will pay for his crimes," she vowed coldly. "Thank you, Selaina." She then walked away and stepped into the room where Ryder had been placed. She moved toward him to ensure he was okay. His face was softer in sleep, and she could recognize the boy that she had known as a child. She couldn't imagine the evil that he had done while he was infected and working with Varone. She knew it was going to be a long road for him when he woke and he could feel guilt and shame again. For the boy that she had known, she would help him as much as she could. She left the room, closing the door silently behind her. Tristan stood in the hallway waiting for her.

"You've had a rough day; how are you doing with all of it?" he asked gently.

"I'm okay, really. I'm ready, and it's far past time that I take care of Varone after all that he's done." She told Tristan about the conversation with Selaina.

"Oh, God, I'm so sorry, Alex." He wrapped his arms around her and she let herself lean into his strength for a moment before pushing away from him.

"We need the angels here now. Please call them down; they may not be prepared for me yet."

"They see the future don't they? I think they probably know you're here."

"No, they can't know I'm here. They have never been able to see the offspring of other angels. Some kind of built-in protection so that we can't be used in their political games unless we seek them."

"You're ready for the politics then? Because once we call them into battle, they will know that you're here."

"Yes. I know who I am now. Call them."

"I will call once we reach the outpost. We will be meeting our allies there." She followed him to the balcony. He spread his onyx wings wide in preparation for the flight. With a thought her own wings appeared, and she stretched her shoulder blades to get accustomed to the weight of them. He ran his eyes over her wings in awe. Then he turned, and they both took to the air.

Chapter Nine: Take the Skies

Tristan filled her in on the strategies during the flight to Canyon Tower. The witches were holed up in Central Tower and would raise the city's circle of protection before the first attack. Canyon Tower was located at the farthest reach of the city on the edge of a cliff. From there the ground dropped away, leaving a crater several thousand feet long. The protective circle around the city began at the cliff, arching over the rest of the city. The witches would stay out of the fight in order to keep the populace safe, but a main focus for their defense would be to destroy the warlocks quickly. The warlocks would be working to unravel the threads of the spells protecting the city.

Ground forces consisting of trained humans, some of the shapeshifters, and those who could not take to the skies would fight against the legion of lower-level demons, young vampires, and other ground enemies in the valley. The Draigkin, Angels, flying shapeshifters, and the light Fae would take to the skies to face the high level demons, dark Fae, and warlocks. They reached the tower and landed on the steepest balcony. Tristan sent the thought out to the angels and one appeared.

The figure on the balcony was beautiful. Androgynous features in a three piece suit and tie suggested that the angel was male. He

131

looked at Tristan, and then his eyes slid to Alex. He became unnaturally still when their eyes met. The widening of his pupils was the only thing that gave away his shock.

"I see that circumstances have changed. Are you infected?" his voice was deep but melodious.

"No, I'm not infected," she answered.

"Very good." He looked around, noticing which tower they were on, looked up to the sky, and paused as though he were listening to something. Then he looked back at them.

"It appears our timeline has changed. The enemy is very close now."

"Yes, our allies have almost arrived. We are assembling now," Tristan told him.

"Very good. The angels will be here momentarily. They are preparing for the battle now. We have never been taken off guard like this before. We saw it beginning a few more days from now. It is… disconcerting that we were incorrect."

"You could not have known of my presence, and I believe I am the cause of the attack being pushed forward," Alex said.

"Yes, I believe you are. I must go and prepare. I shall return momentarily." He looked at her for a second and stepped forward with his hand outstretched. She placed her hand in his. "I respectfully request your accompaniment. We will prepare you for the fight ahead."

Alex glanced back at Tristan. His jaw was clenched. *I must, they are part of me. I'll be back soon*, she sent to him. He nodded once in acceptance and walked inside as she turned back the angel.

In a blink of her eyes she was somewhere else. It appeared to be an armory, so large that she couldn't see where it ended; it just seemed to grow past her vision to infinity. Silver and gold armor hung along the walls and knives, bows, and swords were piled on tables all around them. There were so many angels.

They were all hauntingly beautiful, and they had all stopped in the middle of their preparations to stare at her. The silence was unnerving, but Alex could not show that she was intimidated. She was aware of how weakness could be used against her in the kind of politics that the angels played. Those politics were written in her own DNA.

She inclined her head with a slight smile, stood back up straight, and casually walked to the nearest table and began to choose her weapons. She could feel the satisfaction emanating off the angel who brought her here and the slow spreading of interest among all of the other host.

The angel by her side watched as she picked up and discarded several beautiful bows. As the other angels went back to their preparations and conversations, with an occasional glance in her direction, he leaned toward her and said, "Very well done," so that only she could hear him. "I am Erris. It is a pleasure to meet you. Pray tell me, what may I call you?"

"Alexandria." She picked up a bow that tingled as it settled into her palm, letting her know that it was a perfect fit. She then went to the swords and searched through them until she felt that tingle again. She lifted a beautifully made silver sword with rubies inset in the pommel looking like blood dripping down. Erris began to search through the weapons also as he asked, "Was your mother or your father an angel?"

Alex slid the sword into its scabbard with a snap and turned to him. "Thank you for bringing me here, but do not think that you have any control over me. I am not your tool or your specimen to dissect. I am also aware of how this works. Your rudeness in asking that was a test of my understanding and is an insult to my intelligence of who and what I am." She stared hard at him, and he held his hands up in surrender.

"You are correct and I apologize for my behavior. I have never met an offspring of the immortal pairs. The curiosity must be understandable though, correct? Please forgive me," he said sincerely.

She turned to the armor on the wall. She opened her mind and grabbed the pieces that were meant for her. "I forgive you," she said and felt his genuine relief. "If I decide to trust you, then I will answer your curiosity." She quickly put her armor on and arranged her weapons.

As she finished buckling her breastplate into place, her Focus peeked around her bicep to look up into her eyes. The angels near her jumped in shock at the movement. Her Focus reached one forearm out and pressed its claw to the breastplate. It glowed brightly for a second and then appeared normal. Her Focus relaxed back into place, and she knew that it had changed the armor to be able to grow with her form if she needed to change into that shape. She felt the curiosity around her spark, but she ignored it. Erris returned to her side as a trumpet rang out with a haunting call to arms. He touched her hand, and they were gone.

...

Everyone was in place and the air was thick with excitement and fear. The cry went up as the scouts reported that the dark Fae had burst through the Unseelie tunnels and taken to the air. Thousands of demons had stampeded into sight in the valley. The howls of the wolves and roars of the big cats and bears went up in a spine-tingling cacophony as they prepared to charge to meet them.

The Draigkin front line hovered in the sky above the ground forces, and the officers and generals were to either side of the battlefield surrounded in their camouflage. Tristan and his personal Guard were with them. The first wave of the enemy had just flown into sight when the angels appeared, their powerful wings pumping in sync to keep the line steady as they notched their arrows.

They were glorious and terrifying as they appeared in the sky above the Draigkin force. There were so many of them that Tristan couldn't even begin to guestimate the number. Right at the front was Alex. Tristan's dragon screamed inside of him to go to her and take her somewhere safe, away from the battle, but he fought the desire down. She was strong and beautiful, and he had to allow her to take a stand and prove herself. It was the only way that she could find peace with the past and become the leader that she was destined to be. He tore his focus away from her and let the excitement of battle rage through him.

The Draigkin sped forward to slam into the first wave of the enemy while the angels let loose volley after volley of arrows tipped with angel fire. The sound of screams, roars, steel meeting silver, ripping flesh, and magic burst in the air. The light Fae joined the melee, and the first wave was decimated quickly. The next wave crested before a breath could be taken. They were slightly stronger than the first wave. Tristan sent the call to all of his generals to begin to flank. They would not reveal themselves until after the cannon fodder was gone and the real evil arrived.

Wave after wave crashed into them before the Generals of Mirgrash arrived with the warlocks. As the frontline continued to fight, Tristan and his Generals took off after the warlocks who had immediately flown to the perimeter of the circle around the city. Magic surrounded the circle and began to eat through the woven threads of the spell.

As warlock after warlock died in blood and screams, the others began to throw spells to protect the ones still working on destroying the circle. Tristan dodged a blast of icy rage that would have frozen him in place for a few precious seconds. He switched to his full dragon form and latched onto the warlock that had thrown it with his fore claws. As the warlock screamed in rage and pain, Tristan snapped his jaws over his enemy's head and ripped it off. He spit the head out of his mouth as the warlock's body plummeted toward the ground, and he then took off to continue fighting the remaining warlocks.

Chapter Ten: The Shadows

Alex let loose her arrows, hitting an enemy with each one for what felt like seconds but was in reality a couple of hours as the sun moved higher in the sky. Once the host of angels ran out of arrows, they sped into the fray. Alex hacked and slashed into the enemy with her sword, pushing through them with ease. She slashed through one of the demons in front of her, an evil-looking mash up of a vulture and bearlike creature, when everything around her paused. Sound cut off, and the blood spray froze in the air surrounding her.

She turned and saw Selaina beside her. "What are you doing?" she asked, the blood rage still pumping hard through her.

"You have to go after Varone. Once you take him out the enemy will lose their direction and run back to the dark holes from which they crawled."

She was right, Alex could see it. She sent her awareness out, focusing on the dark void that would indicate his location. When she found him, Selaina disappeared and the sounds and movement around her came crashing back deafeningly. Alex took off like a bullet, wrapping her camouflage around herself. She flew to the other side of the battlefield, dodging the enemy so as not to give herself away.

Varone was concealed in the shadows of the forest, but she could make out his silhouette easily. She made sure to approach with no sound so that he couldn't disappear back to his own realm. She slammed into him full force, pinning his form to the nearest tree with her powerful claws. She dropped her camouflage as she sank her claws through him and into the tree behind him.

The moment her claws touched him, he screamed in agony. Where her claws touched, the shadows peeled back. She poured power into the claws holding him, and the shadows burst into ash all around them. What was left looked like a human, but she knew it was not.

He was hyperventilating as he stared in shock at the pale skin of his arms. She released him and went back to her natural form as she drew out her blade. She felt him try to ghost away and saw the desperate denial in his eyes when it didn't work.

"This is for the innocents that you have killed, corrupted, and manipulated. It's for the evil you've brought to this world and others. This is for Sierra. For my mother and for all of my kin in Ganeska." She slammed the blade directly into his heart with all of her strength, and roughly yanked it back out of him. As he sunk to the ground she knelt there in front of him. "You lose," she whispered.

He tried to breathe and coughed up bright red arterial blood. "Your home," he whispered and coughed again as he fell on his side.

"How would le… letting you… live then… help me now?" He coughed again. "She … won the lo… long game." He tried to get another breath as he began to choke on his blood. He was gone in seconds, his eyes glazing over as the light in them blew out.

She heard Selaina's voice from a long distance away. "He always did talk too much. Even in death he couldn't keep his mouth shut. Thanks for the Crown, sweetie." Alex felt rage boil up and spill over to no avail as Selaina was gone and already back in her Shadow realm. Alex screamed to the sky, pouring out her rage in a long roar from deep in her soul.

The sounds of war began to fade as the enemy retreated quickly.

…

The clean-up took longer than the battle. They dug through the bodies strewn across the valley to find their comrades for proper burials. Once that was done, the Draigkin and the angels purified the area with their fire. The blue, green, and orange flames burned for days, turning the bodies of enemies to ash and the whole valley into a burnt-out shell.

As much as it felt like the battle had centered only around them, Alex learned that battles had raged like this around the world. Once

Varone was destroyed, all the monsters had disappeared back into the shadows and there had been no more whisper of them.

Many hearth cities had been destroyed, and so many lives had been snuffed out. It was unimaginably sad. Even the knowledge of how many they had saved couldn't contain the despair. The citizens had become accustomed to the new cities and were working together to create the governments and laws that would work for each individual area. Trade routes were set up, and everything was operating well so far.

Alex stood on Tristan's balcony staring down at the humanity bustling below. He walked out to stand beside her quietly. She had filled him in on what had happened. He reached out and took her hand in his. She could feel that he wanted to bring up what had happened between them before the battle.

She swallowed hard and faced him. He waited patiently, just watching her. "You do understand why I have to do this, don't you?" she asked quietly.

"I do. I hate the danger you will be putting yourself in, but I understand. You know if you need me, I will find a way to get to you, even if I have to enter the political games of the angels," He vowed.

She stepped forward and hugged him tightly. "You have plenty on your plate for now. Helping the humans with rebuilding and restructuring is a big job." She stepped back. "I won't be alone, but if I need you I will call. I promise." Tristan clenched his fists as Toby walked onto the balcony.

Alex knew that the portal had closed after Selaina had sent the Nephilim and the plague into Ganeska. Otherwise the Nephilim would have left and destroyed the earth, thereby messing up her plans. Only those that were from Ganeska could enter now that it had been locked, and she needed backup. Ryder was all she had.

He had awakened just the day before from the healing sleep that he had engulfed him. He had been almost inconsolable. Alex had removed his memories of his time under Varone's command until he was ready to handle the guilt that would come with it. It would take time for him to gain his personality back with no memory of his life after the age of seven, when he had followed her out of Ganeska.

With a rustle of wings, Erris appeared on the balcony. "The angels are ready. Once you open the portal from inside Ganeska, they will be able to enter."

"Remind them that they are not to harm the Misakin even though they will fight. They are only to subdue the Misakin, but the Nephilim must be destroyed."

He nodded quickly, "We await your command." He smiled and disappeared, the sound of his wings fading quickly.

Tristan lifted her hand to his lips. After a kiss along her knuckles he released her fingers. "Until we meet again."

Ryder stilled and narrowed his eyes in anger toward Tristan. She would have to deal with that later.

"Until then," she answered softly. Then she turned to Ryder, "Time to go."

To be continued...